BOOK SUMMARY

E merald Greed is an adventure set in the Pantanal, vast, inhospitable wetlands in the center of South nerica at the headwaters of the Rio Paraguay. This book, in the early 1990's, tells of the emerald trade, cocaine uggling and of politics as practiced in Brazil. The ry begins with Jack Tate in Rio de Janeiro, working to stablish the industry contacts he had prior to leaving for ica to trade in the "blood diamonds" that were fueling Angolan Civil War. This African venture which ended Zairian prison left him destitute and therefore desperate ugh to head off into the Brazilian hinterlands in search he fabled Borba Mine, knowing that Joaquim Fontes, geologist who re-discovered it, and another gem dealer to find him have both disappeared. As the story unfolds oes a romance between Jack and Joaquim's daughter, isa, who eventually leads him to the mine where their t begins.

EMERALD GREED

Brian Ray Brewer

Library of Congress Control Number: 2021907397

HARDBACK: 978-1-955347-11-2
PAPERBACK: 978-1-955347-10-5
EBOOK: 978-1-955347-12-9

For orders and inquiries, please contact:
1-888-404-1388
www.goldtouchpress.com
book.orders@goldtouchpress.com

Printed in the United States of America

Dedication

For Silviane.

Acknowledgments

I would like to thank Laurie Dove, acute of ear and eye, for her help in editing this and other manuscripts, and I would also like to thank Zach Hunter whose persistence helped bring this book to print. Finally, I must thank my wife, Silviane, for her continued patience, her support and her beatific presence that anchors me in all weather.

Prologue

Chico Borba should have been exhausted, but he wasn't. And he should have felt pain from the wicked gash torn wide above his left eye, but he didn't. He felt elation and glory.

It had been an auspicious day. Two weeks before, Dom Pascoal Moreira Cabral, the *comandante* of the *bandeira*, had made him a lieutenant as a reward for the bravery and ability he displayed along their 1,600-kilometer trek from São Paulo. With the promotion came a mission—he was to strike south away from the main body of the *bandeira* in search of a band of Parecis Indians who escaped their initial assault, and that morning he had found and defeated them. The Indians fought desperately and bravely but in vain, and with the capture of their chief came their surrender and something even more important.

Chico Borba looked down at what he held in his hand— the key to a captaincy most likely, he thought, grinning. It was beautiful, and he would present it to the *comandante* along with the 70 Indian slaves he had captured. He had wrenched it from the neck of the Parecis chief after personally bringing him low in battle with a well-placed stroke of his musket butt. He stared down into the peaceful green of the long, hexagonal crystal almost perfect in symmetry. It was a magnificent emerald. And where it came from there were sure to be more. Fame and wealth were his, if only he could find the mine.

He walked out of his tent and across the makeshift camp to the tree where the chief was being flayed by a relentless *bandeirante*. Chico Borba motioned for the soldier to stop.

"Has our friend decided to talk yet?"

"*Não, Senhor*. He only laughs, like he did an hour ago when you left."

Chico Borba nodded and stepped up to the bound chief. As a half-breed, the son of a Portuguese trader and an Indian squaw, he spoke fluent Tupi-Guarani, a language common to most of the tribes that roamed the Central Brazilian plains.

He leaned in close and spoke, "You must tell me where to find your emerald mine, *Meu Amigo*, or I will be forced to torture your people to death, one by one, beginning with you. You don't have a choice. We will find out where it is one way or another, so save yourself and your tribe."

"For what?" asked the chief. "For a chance to die as slaves in the mines of our fathers? You have our gold, but you will never have our green stones. They are for Parecis chiefs, not the bastard sons of the Portuguese."

Chico Borba eyed the Indian calmly. He knew that he would die soon, and he didn't seem likely to give up his secret. *Let him die with it*, thought Borba. *I'll burn him alive for all the rest to see, and I'll have the mine's location soon after.*

"Pile wood under him," he ordered curtly to the *bandeirante* holding the whip. "And have all the other Indians gathered close around this tree. Send word to me when you are done. I'll be in my tent."

The *bandeirante* saluted roughly, and Borba walked back across the camp, wondering what the life of a rich man would be like.

*   *   *   *

Chico Borba addressed the Indians hobbled and bound and ringed in a rough circle around him. "You are defeated. You are now our slaves, and we own you and all that you possess. This slave before you was unwilling to cooperate with his masters. He wouldn't tell us of the home of the green stones, and now you must see what happens to slaves who don't cooperate. This will be the fate of all of you if you don't tell me where to find the stones."

Borba thrust a rude torch into the limbs and brush piled high beneath the chief, and they caught instantly in a fog of crackling sparks and rising flame.

As the first yellow tongues licked the feet of the bound chief, he screamed in agony and began laughing hysterically. He let the flames reach his burning calves before he spoke his prophesy through his pained and choking laughter.

"Fool!" he cackled. "You will never find the home of the green stones now! Only the chief of the Parecis knows the secret of the green stones, and I am dead. You will never sneak into the waters, into the mouth of the caiman and into the home of the Bororo. You couldn't make it even if you knew where to look. Only the son of a Parecis chief is brave enough and tough enough to make the journey. Take my stone and take my soul with it. I will be a curse on the head of the Portuguese. I will drive you from our land and back across the ocean. You will be weak and puny. I curse you..."

His prophesy ended in a long, unbroken series of screams until the fire consumed him.

Chapter One

The taxi moved slowly down Avenida Vieira Souto with the morning traffic. The air was already hot and was filled with the angry honking of *Cariocas* peeved that they were headed to work and would be deprived of the sensual pleasures of Rio de Janeiro until evening. Jack gazed out the window at the sun rising above the beach. Joggers were out in force, and here and there, bikini-clad girls were already swaying along the beach they'd made famous. *I'll never tire of coming here*, he thought as his taxi turned left, away from the beach and into the heart of Ipanema. After driving a few blocks, his taxi turned onto *Rua Visconde de Pirajá*, a major thoroughfare that paralleled the beach.

"*Aqui, por favor.*" Jack motioned toward a walk-up entrance next to a chic jewelry store fronting the boulevard. The driver pulled over and said with a smile, "Tweenty *dólares,* my friend."

"*O que?*" questioned Jack. "What is this? Let me see your price table."

The driver lost his smile on being answered in Portuguese and reluctantly reached up to his sun visor to pull it down. Jack checked the number registered on the meter against the corresponding price on the table—240,000 *cruzeiros reais*, a little less than four dollars that day. Jack counted out a large pile of bills and checked it carefully: every time he returned to Brazil, he had to re-learn the currency—it had either changed entirely, or had gained or lost several zeros. Anything of value was always priced in dollars. The country's paper money blew down the streets without anyone taking notice, even in this city full of beggars and homeless children. It became totally worthless within a few years of being printed. Jack paid the driver, now grim upon seeing that his passenger couldn't be cheated. He picked up his briefcase and stepped out into the street. He rang the *interfone* at the walk-up entrance and stood back in full view of the closed-circuit camera.

"*Alô*?" crackled out from the speaker.

"I'm Jack Tate, here to see Itzhak Blum."

"*Um momento.*"

He stood and waited, watching the street, already alive with people at that early hour. In his business one had to be wary in a town like Rio. He never made solid appointments with those he dealt with, preferring instead to pop in at any odd hour when least expected. This prevented him from being set up, but even so, he always kept an open eye for potential robbers—the city was full of them. Young thugs were everywhere, as were bands of child criminals. Worst of all, however, were unscrupulous policemen armed with the power of the law and the threat of time in a Brazilian prison, which was enough to empty the pockets of the bravest tourist. It was the police in Rio who he feared most.

With the sound of heavy deadbolts sliding clear, the door swung open to reveal a small, wrinkled man whose keen eyes sparkled out from under a 10X magnifying visor which was flipped up on his head like the bill of a baseball cap.

"Jack, hello! It's good to see you, *amigo*. It's been some time. Have you become so rich in your business that you no longer have time to visit an old friend, the man who made you such a grand success?"

They shook hands and embraced.

"No, it's not that at all, Itzhak. I've been dying to come back to Rio and visit you, but business took me elsewhere. People haven't been buying emeralds as they were in the early eighties, and your prices never helped much either. I would guess I was in Columbia by looking at what you people are charging around here. I'm having to struggle to make a living these days."

"The day I see you struggle to make a living will be the day that I see fish dance in the street. I had hoped to see you and Heiner both last year, but did I see you? Did I hear from you? No! Not even a card. It's not just business between us, Jack. You young men are like family to me, and it does an old heart bad to be abandoned so..."

The elder smiled up at his friend, then took his arm to lead him up the stairs to his shop.

"So tell me, Jack, what have you found that has kept you from our shores so long?"

"You can keep a secret, can't you, Itzhak?"

"You ask this question of me, your mentor?"

"Sorry, just don't spread this around: if I'm found out it could hurt me in the trade—I was in Angola for a couple of years buying contraband diamonds and selling them to the DeBeers cartel through an intermediary. The civil war flashed up again, though, so it got a little too hot to stay."

"You like the dangerous life, don't you?"

"I'm not the one who lives in Rio."

"True, so true. My paradise isn't much of a paradise anymore." The old man's eyes dimmed and his shoulders sagged. "When I came here from Vienna in the late thirties, I came with nothing but hopes and dreams for a better life, and I found one here. The people were not like my people had become. Nobody begrudged a Jew here. I was just a little man with a funny accent, European and therefore cultured—someone to invite to dinner once in a while. I fit right in, so I started a small lapidary business with little fear of having it taken from me. Business boomed during the war years. Women in America started buying our colored stones—amethyst, topaz, citrine, others—as substitutes for more traditional gems like rubies and sapphires that were unavailable because of the war. I pinned my hopes on Brazil when I was young and it paid off. But what does hope bring a youth just starting out in business here today? It gives him a chance to despair even more when he realizes that his hope was a delusion that he framed for himself. This country offers nothing to its children anymore. How could that have happened?"

Itzhak paused, started to say more, then checked himself. He looked up and smiled.

"Forgive an old man his mutterings, Jack. There is always hope for the young and hope for the future. The horrors I escaped in Europe are long past and maybe this economic disaster here will pass also. It must, one day... At least the dictatorship has ended and we have a good-hearted president. He spent the last four years doing everything in his power to turn this country around, but was always blocked by the monied elite who won't give up even a little, not even to save their own country. I hope he wins re-election this year. Maybe this election will bring more like him into the senate and congress, so he can make a change. But I don't think so. The way it looks now, we'll probably lose him, too. That glad-handing, lying, populist Fonseca is ahead in the poles. God help us if he wins. He'll steal the plumbing out of the *Palácio da Alvorada* the day he moves in.

"But enough of this. I won't speak anymore of politics. I haven't the time. Now I have to concentrate on separating you from all of your valuable dollars! Let's go into my office."

They walked past two armed guards to another door that Itzhak unlocked. Then they entered a large, well-lit room where several men were polishing gemstones on lapping scaifes and where others were cutting rough crystals to size with bench-mounted gem saws. From there, they passed into another room where two young women in lab coats were seated at a table grading gemstones with loupes and sorting them into various piles. The blues, reds, pinks and greens of the stones sparkled richly in the cool, white light of the grading room. Another armed guard stood in a corner next to the open door of a walk-in safe. At the end of this room, they stepped up a small staircase that led to a windowed office with views of the entire operation and of the street four stories below.

Itzhak sat behind his worn and cluttered desk and motioned for his friend to take a seat in a facing chair.

"So, how's your retail business going?" asked Jack. "The global recession hurt you much?"

"Well, you know our economy here in Brazil has been dismal for fifteen years, but the rich somehow get richer while the poor and the middle class suffer on with even less. Hyperinflation is good for those with money in the bank but is hard on the salaried classes. Since my clientele are the—how do you say it—the well-heeled? Yes, since my patrons are the well-heeled, I do manage to survive in my own humble way."

They both smiled.

"My exports have been down, though, for quite some time. Perhaps my wealthy young American friend has come here to change my luck, now that he has returned from his plundering of Africa."

The old jeweler stretched back in his chair, touched his chin with the tips of both forefingers and gazed at the man across from him, ready for business.

"So, Jack, what can I interest you in today? I have excellent aquamarine up to eighty carats, and we have cut some fine rubellite tourmaline in large sizes. I've even managed to get my hands on some Paraíba neon, greens and blues, but I can't let it go cheaply, Jack. It's very hot and very rare at the moment. The mine is already almost played out. On Paraíba, I'm afraid I should to stick a friend as dear as you, but I'll do the best I can. Perhaps some imperial topaz? I'm the only one in this city with a decent stock."

"Sorry, Itzhak, this trip I'm only buying emerald, fine emerald, the best I can get. I, too, have a few wealthy clients, though surely not as wealthy as yours. I can move as much emerald as you can get me, from one to five carats in the fine to extra-fine ranges, but it's got to be good. Save your junk for the tourists and the Home Shopping Network."

"Do you really supply them?" asked Jack, somewhat amazed that his friend would bother to export goods of such low quality.

The jeweler only smiled. Then he pressed a button on his intercom.

"*Pois não, Senhor.*"

"Silvia, *por favor*, bring me our best emeralds in the larger sizes."

"*Sim, Seu Itzhak.*"

He released the button.

"Maybe you aren't aware, Jack, because you've been off adventuring and haven't been involved in this trade in a while—our production in larger emeralds has been lacking in color the past few years. I have very nice stones, magnificent stones, up to around a carat, but they just haven't been mining much in the way of large stones. Have you been to Columbia?"

"I just spent two weeks in Bogotá, but it's no good there now. Drug money is snapping up all the good stuff before it leaves the mines. I guess that's one way the cartels launder their money. They're buying all the good stuff at ridiculously inflated prices and driving up the price on all that's left. Not even the Japanese are buying much there now, but I don't know if it's because of overpricing or because of the recession in Japan. For me, though, Columbia is priced way out of the market, and the stones there aren't any better than what's being mined anywhere else."

"Is it rough for you Americans in Columbia because of your government's attack on the drug rings?"

"Not for me. I just speak Portuguese and tell everybody I'm Brazilian."

Itzhak gasped. "Americans masquerading as Brazilians! I should die soon. My God, this world's gone crazy. Maybe I shall see fish dance in the street after all!"

They were laughing as a girl brought in several trays of loose, cut emeralds. She lay them out on the desk in front of Jack and left, returning a moment latter with a pot of fresh espresso. Jack pulled out a jeweler's loupe and tweezers from his pocket and began to examine the stones. He frowned over the parcel and as he examined the stones his frown intensified. Itzhak watched him carefully almost as if measuring the metal from which he were cast.

Jack looked up after only a few minutes. "Is this it, Itzhak? Is this the best you have?"

"Have you been to anybody else and looked at their stock?" asked the old jeweler.

"Sure, Itzhak. I've seen everybody in Rio and in Teófilo Otoni. I always save you, the best, for last. Nobody has anything much better than commercial grade stones. I can't sell these. They just aren't good enough, not for exclusive trade. I'd ruin my reputation mounting stones like these."

"Well, then why don't you buy halvers or three-quarters?"

"I need big stones, for one customer in particular. I deal with an eccentric old lady in Houston who's loaded with oil money. She's an emerald fanatic. Almost every important emerald I ever bought from you was on order from her. When I got back from Angola, she was there ready to buy, but she's savvy and knows her emeralds. She wouldn't accept these. No way.

Come on, Itzhak, you must have something for me. I know you—you always manage to come up with what the others cannot. What about the stock for your retail business? Fleece me if you want, but get me some stones. If you can't, I guess I'll have to go to Zambia or Zimbabwe to see what I can find there, but I'll tell you, I don't really relish the thought of going back to Africa, not now. I have memories of that continent that I'd rather forget."

The old man rocked back in his chair, stroked his chin and regarded his young friend carefully. "Tell me about Angola, Jack."

"Not much to tell, Itzhak. It was hot. It stank, and it was dangerous. We had the police, the Army and De Beers after us all the time, but there were too many people working the fields for them to control things. And if you were caught, you could always bribe your way out of trouble in an instant. Since I'm a gemologist and know my diamonds, I was as valuable to the *garimpeiros* as the stones they were finding— finding, Itzhak! Not mining. Angola is an alluvial field— diamonds are sprinkled all over the ground there like salt on a pretzel . I was the money man, and I knew what was what, so the *garimpeiros* took care of me. It was miserable there, but it was worth it. I was getting rich right to the end when UNITA wouldn't honor the new election and started the civil war up again. All hell broke loose. I was lucky to get out with my life, and that's about all I have left."

He sighed, then continued. "I got picked up by the Army in Zaire when I crossed the border illegally. They took everything, well almost everything—I did manage to get out with a few of my choice diamonds."

"How?"

"I had to swallow them. Not a pleasant memory. Anyway, I got picked up by a Zairian border patrol that wasn't very happy to find an American with a fortune in diamonds sneaking through the brush. They took my inventory, beat me, threw me in jail, and finally, when they realized they couldn't get anything else from me, they let me go. I'm sure I would have probably done some serious time, but the Army major didn't want to turn my diamonds over to the police. I don't know why he didn't order me shot, unless he found the thought of getting caught with American blood on his hands a little bit too risky.

"I'm practically ruined, Itzhak. I lost two years' worth of diamonds, all paid for with money that I had been saving over the previous eight years—all contraband and all taken from me when I crossed an international border illegally during a civil war. It's gone, all of it, but at least I'm still alive."

"You are alive, Jack. Don't discount that. Fortunes come and go, but this life we lead comes only once. My family was wealthy in Vienna, you know. We owned a string of jewelry stores. Our main store was right on the Ringstrasse, a block away from the Staatsopera! My brother and I had a wonderful, privileged life until our parents were killed in a streetcar accident in 1933 and we inherited control of the business. We found out that we, as Jews, were losing our place in the community. Our parents had shielded us, kept us insulated from the worst while they were alive, but we found out quickly that things weren't going to be easy for young Jewish businessmen in Austria. It got worse for us by the year, and I fled in 1938 with the forced annexation of Austria by Germany. I saw the way things were turning and chanced poverty over staying. My brother, though, did not. He was older and much more involved in running the business. It was his life, and he couldn't let it go. There was too much of him in it. Now I'm alive, and he is not. He didn't die in a concentration camp, though, not Felix. He held off the Nazis until he ran out of bullets and died in his home with a gun in his hand. He was stubborn and tough 'til the end."

"I'm sorry to hear that. I didn't know."

"Thanks, my young friend, but don't worry. It was long ago. I'm just glad that you got out of Africa in one piece."

"I am too, Itzhak, but I sure wish I had somehow managed to get out with more of my money. This client I have in Houston was easily fifty percent of my business and used to be mine exclusively, but since I was away so long, she found other jewelers. She's looking for a matched suite of fifteen perfect, five-carat emeralds for a necklace I designed for her a few years ago, and I promised I could get them for her. If I can deliver and make the sale, I'll get her back, and with a sale like that my reputation will soar. If not, I'll have to start again from scratch."

Itzhak again inspected his friend as if he were measuring him against some task.

After a time, he rose from behind his desk. "I think I have something you should see."

He walked to the windows of his office and closed their many curtains. When the room was sheltered from the view of all others, he pulled back his chair and rolled up the carpet beneath it, revealing a floor safe that he quickly spun open. He withdrew a display tray covered with a jewel-cleaning cloth and set the tray on his desk before his young friend.

"Take a look at these, Jack." He swept away the cloth like a magician and unveiled a suite of magnificent large emeralds that shone in the cool of his desk lamp like crystalline puddles of pure sylvan light.

Jack sucked in a breath of shocked surprise and immediately hunched over them with his loupe held to his eye. With his tweezers, he picked up each gem in turn and examined them closely. They were all near-perfect and almost free of inclusions under a 10X magnifier, from the smallest half carat to the largest, which must have weighed fifteen carats. All were easily VVS—the highest grade on the clarity scale for emeralds—and their color was excellent, very slightly bluish green, the most sought-after color. They were beautiful and very, very valuable. Jack knew he was looking at least half a million—wholesale! And below the array of artfully cut stones was a hexagonal crystal. It was perfect in symmetry and over three centimeters long, uncut yet unquestionably gorgeous, even in the rough.

Jack had never seen such emeralds. He sat up after his long examination and smiled to his friend.

"I'm astounded, Itzhak. That's the nicest lot of emerald I've ever seen. They're exquisite. Where on earth did they come from?"

"You wouldn't believe me if I told you," answered the old man, who seemed hesitant to discuss the origin of the stones.

"Try me."

"They're from the Borba mine."

"Sure, Itzhak, sure, and that gold pen in your pocket came from the gift shop in El Dorado. Now seriously, where did you get them?"

Jack picked up the fifteen-carat stone and examined it through his loupe. He lost himself in its sea of green.

"I'm serious, Jack. Those stones are from the Borba mine."

Jack set the stone down and looked at his friend. "Come on, you can't mean that. The Borba mine's just a legend, like the lost city of Atlantis or Ponce de Leon's Fountain of Youth."

"Then where did the Heart of Brazil come from?"

"I don't know, Itzhak, maybe Columbia or India. It didn't come from here—the color's too good for a stone that size. And it didn't come from some mysterious mine in the jungle wrapped in mystery, either. I suppose you think that Martians built the pyramids in Egypt, too."

Jack laughed. "Now come on and tell me where you got these."

"The man who brought those to me says he found the Borba mine, and I believe he did. I know him, Jack, from at least twenty years ago. He used to own a share in the Salininha deposits up in Bahia back in the late 60s and early 70s. He sold his claims just before the mines started playing out and went out West to search for the Borba mine. I never heard of him again until six months ago, when he brought me the stones you're looking at."

"You really think there is a Borba mine, Itzhak?" asked Jack with diminishing skepticism.

"If the man that brought me these stones believes there is, then so do I. He's no crackpot, Jack. He used to be a professor of geology and cartography at the *Universidade Federal* here in Rio. In the trade, he was known as The Professor. He was a very, very intelligent man."

"You talk of him as if he's dead."

"I think he might be. He was supposed to contact me in July and let me know if he had anything for me, but I never heard from him. In fact, I only saw him the day he brought me these. He had changed greatly from the days I knew him. He was rugged and confident in the old days, one of those people you occasionally meet who thinks he can do anything, and you believe he can. But when he sold me these stones, he was very nervous. He was afraid of something, but wouldn't say.

The Professor had done well in Bahia in the old days and lived well with his family in Leblon. His wife was the daughter of a doctor and was beautiful, and he had two handsome boys who were sure to grow into lady-killers. As long as I knew him, he always spoke of the Borba mine. He thought there was truth behind the legend, and he always dreamed of finding the riches it contained. Do you know the legend, Jack?"

"No, not really. Just something about an Indian mine deep in the Amazon where the Heart of Brazil came from, a mine that disappeared long ago, swallowed up by the jungle."

"Well, that's not quite the legend. Let me tell you. In 1719, Pascoal Moreira Cabral led a *bandeira* out of São Paulo, heading west to hunt for Indian slaves. A *bandeira* was a paramilitary band of marauding pioneers, called *bandeirantes*. They were named *bandeiras* because each of the groups had its own *bandeira*, or flag, to which the *bandeirantes* pledged allegiance. This *bandeira* discovered gold in the Rio Cuiabá, founded the city of Cuiabá, the capital of the state of Mato Grosso, and then started panning with the help of several hundred Indian slaves. While he was gathering slaves, one of Cabral's henchmen, a sadistic half-breed named Francisco 'Chico' Borba who thought he

13

could make himself whiter with every Indian he killed, took an emerald from an Indian chief. He tortured the chief, but couldn't get him to tell where the mine was. Finally, Borba burned the chief as an object lesson in cooperation for the other Indians. As the chief burned, he laid a curse upon the Portuguese, claiming that his soul would dwell in the emerald; he would make the Portuguese weak and force them from Brazil. He also said something about the mine being in caiman-filled water in the land of the Bororo, another Indian tribe. It was the only information Borba was able to get about the mine, because none of the other thirty Indians he burned knew anything about it. They all claimed that the mine was a secret reserved exclusively for chiefs and their sons. The chief's only son had been killed in battle a few weeks earlier, so no living person knew the location of the mine.

Borba was daunted, but not defeated. He determined that the mine had to lie south in an inhospitable wetland called the Pantanal, which was the water fortress of the fierce Bororo. He then convinced Cabral that he could find the mine. He set out in its search at the head of a hundred men. He was never seen again.

The Viceroy of Brazil, the Count of Subugosa, later confiscated the emerald and sent it to his benefactress, the Queen of Portugal, as a personal gift. She was enthralled by it, named it the Heart of Brazil and placed it in her crown. Then she commissioned another *bandeira* to search for the mine. It met with disaster and was quickly decimated by the Bororo, caimans, snakes and malaria. Of the six hundred men who entered the Pantanal on the Queen's decree, less than a hundred made it out alive. You know, Jack, there may be something to the curse."

"Why, because a bunch of *bandeirantes* caught malaria?"

"No, because a hundred years after the Queen placed the Heart of Brazil in her crown, Brazil was wrested from Portugal by her own great-great grandson who rebelled against his father and declared himself Dom Pedro the First, Emperor of Brazil. As a power in the world, Portugal has been in decline ever since."

"Well, Portugal did fall from the ranks of the world powers quite a while back, that's true. But do you really believe these stones are from the Borba mine, Itzhak?"

"Yes, I believe they are. The Professor knew more about the Borba legend than anyone. He spent years researching it. If you have doubts, look at the gems in front of you."

"I guess you're right," said Jack, taking his time, knowing the negotiation was about to begin in earnest. "That's even better. These stones will be even more valuable with a legend attached. I need to weigh these, of course, but just by looking I'd say they are worth four hundred thousand in U.S. dollars."

"They are far more valuable than that, Jack, and you know it. Save your breath. I can't sell them to you. They're already sold."

Jack looked devastated. "They're sold?"

"Sorry, afraid so. I've already been paid, so don't even bother trying to deal. I'm just holding them now for the owner. If you want more of these, we need to find The Professor ."

"Well then, I guess we'd better get a hold of him. See if he's still alive, for starters. Do you have his phone number?"

"Unfortunately not. I don't think he has a phone. And, while I agree that we must find him…Jack, I'm an old, old man. I don't make long trips anymore. Why don't we make a deal? I'll give you all the information I have about The Professor, and my best guess as to where the mine is, then you and I split the goods you bring back fifty-fifty. I'll front you money if you need it."

"Fifty-fifty, Itzhak? You want me to do all the work and then split the goods with you fifty-fifty? You're crazy. I'll give you a chance at fifteen percent of whatever I bring back."

"Information's not cheap, Jack, not information like this. I want forty."

"Seventeen."

"Thirty."

"Twenty, but you've got to back me financially on my percentage if I'm short."

"Deal."

They shook on it, and Itzhak smiled, remembering the young man he helped train to bargain by stiffing him a few times. "You're tough on me, my young friend," he said.

"Would you have it any other way?"

"No, never. The joy is in the bargain."

"So tell me what you know, Itzhak."

"I don't know much, unfortunately, but here's what I do have." He walked back around his desk and kneeled down to pull a file folder from the floor safe. He stood and handed it to Jack.

Jack opened it, then looked up, frowning. "Is this all you have, Itzhak? Just an address and a fuzzy picture? I'm giving you twenty percent for an address?"

"Don't forget the picture. It's a starting point isn't it? Where would you be without it?"

Jack grimaced at the old man.

"There are a few more things I should tell you. I paid The Professor $250,000 in *cruzeiros reais* for the rough from which I cut these stones. He didn't want to travel with the money, so I deposited it in an account he opened here at Banco do Brasil. I became anxious when I didn't hear from him, so I did a little covert checking and found that in the first two months he withdrew a total of around $5,000 on different occasions in Poconé, the town he lives in. The rest of the money, all of it, was then withdrawn entirely at a branch in Cuiabá a month after the last small withdrawal. It seems strange, doesn't it?"

"Yes, I guess it does. Maybe, he decided to cash out of Brazil. Well, let's see if we can find out. I'll fly out to Cuiabá tonight and should make it to Poconé tomorrow sometime. Is it far from Cuiabá?"

"No, I don't think so, maybe a few hundred kilometers."

"Good, then I'll be there tomorrow morning." Jack threw the folder in his briefcase and stood.

"Jack, there is one other thing that I should tell you."

"What's that, Itzhak?"

"You remember Heiner Klimt, don't you?"

"How could I forget Heiner? That damn German's been a plague to me since I got in this business. He's beaten me out of more deals than I have teeth, and he managed to get out of Angola with his money. What about him?"

"Well, he's the man I sold these stones to."

"Why doesn't that surprise me?"

Jack was disgusted. Once again he'd been beaten by Heiner.

"And he went to Cuiabá a month ago to look for The Professor."

"What!" Jack was livid. "You sold him the same information that you sold me? What is this, Itzahk?"

"He came here first, Jack. He got the first chance at these emeralds and the first chance at finding the mine because he came to me first. I haven't even had a postcard from you in over two years, remember?"

"Sorry." Jack regained his composure and said, "It just seems that I'm always a day late whenever I deal with Heiner."

"Maybe not this time. I'm worried about him and don't know if I should be sending you after him. He called me from Poconé the day he got there and told me that he found The Professor's wife and daughter, but no professor and no sons. That was the last I ever heard from him."

"He's probably shacked up somewhere, celebrating with a friend he made along the way. You know how Heiner is."

"I hope that's it, Jack. I know you two can take care of yourselves, but the interior can even be rougher than Rio when money's involved. I have a bad feeling about this, a very bad feeling."

"Relax, Itzhak. Don't worry about me. I just got back from a civil war. I'll find your professor and his mine. And I'll drag Heiner back if I can find him, but I'll be the one with the sack of stones. I won't let him beat me, not this time."

"I hope you won't, Jack. Heiner was only going to give me fifteen percent."

They both laughed.

"But please be careful and take care of yourself. And take this." The old jeweler opened a drawer and pulled out a loaded pistol, which he handed to his friend.

"Put it in your checked baggage. They never look through it on domestic flights."

Jack reluctantly accepted the gun and put it in his briefcase, hoping he wouldn't need it.

They shook hands. Itzhak was clearly worried.

"Relax, my friend," said Jack as he was leaving "I'll call you from Poconé."

Chapter Two

A rooster tail wake of fine dust puffed up like a contrail and marked Jack's passage as he bumped along the rough dirt road in a third attempt to locate the home of The Professor.

He had been down this road twice before, but never found his turn-off and was forced to backtrack to Poconé to ask for further directions. The address he had, #34 *Rua* 15, looked easy on paper, but it wasn't. The streets at town center were numbered but numbered out of sequence—Fifth Avenue was followed by Seventeenth Street, which was followed by Avenue 1A then Thirteenth Street. After Thirteenth Street, the pavement and street signs ended abruptly, replaced by a nameless and rutted track of red clay.

Jack had followed the intricate and expert instructions of first a gas station attendant and then a grocery store clerk, but both were wildly different and equally wrong . This time he flagged down the mailman, who was at a loss for the street, but who recognized the name of The Professor. He didn't bother with street names, he confided to Jack: he delivered mail to people!

Armed now with a map drawn on the back of a political handbill, Jack was confident that he would find the house that had eluded him for the past two hours—he wanted to be confident, anyway. Turning, as his map suggested, onto the washed-out lane behind a broken windmill to his left, his certainty grew. A shack appeared to his right just as it appeared on the paper, and a kilometer further on, he encountered a rickety wooden bridge that was also marked on the map, but which was in such bad condition that he had to pull over and get out to see if he could safely cross.

While he pondered its splintered, broken planks and weighed his chances of falling through it and into the gully below, a truck rumbled and bounced along behind him honking for him to get out of the way. He stepped clear of the racing truck and marveled as it blew across the narrow one-lane bridge without even slowing down. *If it can make it*, he thought, *well maybe so can I*, but he wasn't very sure. With a resigned shrug, he got in his rented Volkswagen Gol and slowly edged across the beams that creaked and moaned at his passage. A few kilometers on, he found the small white stucco house, more pink than white because of the red dust that blanketed it. This was his destination according to his map, but it lacked the tell-tale number 34. He parked and walked through the desolate, spotty yard up to the door.

The door and the two small windows that fronted the house were open to catch any chance of a stirring breeze in the already scorching heat of the dry, late morning air. He knocked on the door frame and shouted out, "*Alô!*"

A parrot squawked in answer, and soon a thin, middle aged, once-handsome woman peered out from the inner darkness and questioned warily, "What do you want?"

"*Bom dia, Senhora*," replied Jack in a friendly voice. "Is this the house of Professor Fontes?"

"Why? Who wants to know?"

"I do, *Senhora*. My name's Jack Tate. I'm a gem buyer."

"Never heard of you," she mumbled.

"No, I'm sure you haven't. Itzhak Blum sent me here to look for Professor Fontes. Is this his house? Are you *Senhora* Fontes?"

She laughed coldly and answered, "That's right. That's me, Isabella Fontes, once of Leblon, but lately the *dona* of the empire you see stretched out before you!"

She waved a hand around her, pointing at the tiny, run-down house and to the broken-down jumble of flumes and sieves that littered her grassless lawn. Gold mining equipment was heaped everywhere—shovels, pans, screens, a generator, pump and hoses, all of it rusty and in obvious decline. As she laughed, frustration burned in her eyes and the parrot began to squawk and shrill along with her. Momentarily it hopped into view and pulled at her dress with its crescent beak. She bent down and offered her arm as a perch, which the bird gratefully accepted. Then she stood straight and faced her visitor. Her laughter was gone, but her anger remained as she glared at him. She stroked the parrot's green head with a mad glint in her dark brown eyes.

He paused at her reaction, but then continued, "*Senhora* Fontes, Itzhak Blum sent me here to look for your husband. It seems that your husband had promised to meet him some time ago, but never made the trip out to Rio. Itzhak hasn't heard a word from him since."

"Welcome to the club."

"Your husband isn't here?"

"That's right. No husband. No sons. No money. Nothing. Nothing but a miserable past full of false hopes and promises for a bright future, and no future left to me at all—other than growing old in this dismal swamp to see my daughter married off to whatever prospector or scum *caipira* finally wears her down with promises, and who will then get her pregnant out of ignorance and tie her down in this damned hole to live in poverty forever."

Jack was startled by her roughness, but continued pleasantly, "Where can I find your husband, *Dona* Isabella?"

As she stroked her parrot softly, tears welled in her eyes. She blinked them back hard, her anger returning.

She glared up to Jack and answered, "Probably with his idiot sons who were too much like him to have sense enough to get out of here when they could."

"And where are they?" he asked.

"In the river bottom somewhere. Their bones are anyway. The *piranhas* and the *bagres* surely ate the rest of them."

Her hot tears flowed.

"My poor babies. My poor sons. They were so young, more children than men, but they had to be like their father, always like their father, that silly man, the dreamer that they worshipped, and now they're gone from me forever. And he's gone too..."

Her parrot began squawking, so she gently brushed its feathered head and washed it with a teardrop.

Jack wasn't prepared for the uncomfortable situation and didn't know how to react. He put a comforting hand upon her shoulder, which she immediately brushed off. The parrot swung forward to get a piece of him as his hand fell back to his side. It missed, just barely. It flapped its wings and squawked, tilting its head from side to side and bobbing out toward Jack from its perch on her forearm.

"*Calma, Eduardo. Calma!*" She stroked and soothed the bird.

"I'm sorry to hear about your sons, *Dona* Isabella. Your husband and sons are dead?"

"Yes, they're dead. All dead. There's no one here for you to talk to about gems now, so why don't you go away and leave us to mourn in peace?"

She stepped back and was about to close the door.

Jack put a hand on it to stop her. "Please, *Senhora*. Please hear me out. I'm sorry about your family. Perhaps I can help you."

"How are you going to help me? Are you going to take me back to Rio? Are you going to give me back my youth? Are you going to send my daughter to college and get her out of here while she still has a chance at life?"

"I don't know that I can do that, *Senhora*, but we might be able to do business together. About six months ago, your husband sold some emeralds to Itzhak Blum. The emeralds were good, very good, some of the best I've ever seen, and they were very, very valuable. I am interested in buying more of them if you have any."

"I don't have any emeralds, *Gringo*. I don't have anything, except this. Nothing, only this!" She pulled out a pendant that was hidden in her blouse. It was a beautiful stone like the others he saw in Rio, about three carats, cushion cut and set in a simple yet elegant gold and diamond mounting.

Blum's work, he guessed, probably a present The Professor had made for her when he made the sale. He had to see it under a loupe to be sure, but with its depth of even, saturated color and its lack of inclusions, the emerald was top of the list, VVS easy—worth about 45 grand, retail, and he could sell it in an hour in Houston. Stones that good sold themselves. God, if he could only get a dozen more like it, he'd be back in business.

He reached out to examine it, but she pulled it away. Her guard bird craned its neck and uttered a warning squawk.

"*Dona* Isabella, I'd have to look at that to be sure, but I'm guessing that I could give you around twenty-five thousand dollars for your necklace."

"No. Never. It's the only thing I have left of my husband."

She looked into the emerald depths of the crystal, and after a long moment she spoke to it. "You found your mine didn't you, Joaquim. You realized your dream, but it was as much a curse for you as it was for Chico Borba, wasn't it my husband—your whole life spent in its search, and now you're gone on the eve of your great victory. It swallowed you up like it swallowed all the *bandeirantes* before you. Why did you have to be such a believer? Why did you want it so much? Why couldn't you give it up and let us return to Rio and our life? My poor, dear husband. My poor Joaquim..."

She lost herself in stricken reverie while Jack looked on, uneasy.

His heart went out to her, filled with empathy and understanding. He had seen many men consumed by the promise of wealth that a lucky mining strike could bring in Columbia, Africa and here in Brazil. He'd seen men by the thousands risk it all for a chance at millions, but he'd only known a handful that truly struck it rich. More often than not, they fell victim to their emerald greed and returned penniless, or they were buried in the land they worked, some murdered, some starved, some simply worked-out and broken, driven to death by their avarice. He, too, knew the passion and the lust of one dedicated to and trapped in the search of the perfect crystal. He'd had the bug for most of his adult life, and the fact that all his years of hard work had brought little in the long run didn't deter him at all—he was where he was ten years before, but that didn't matter. He could make it all back in an instant if he worked hard and got lucky, and he felt closer to the big one then more than ever before.

This woman was the key. If she would just let him work her mine, they could both be rich. Everything he'd seen from the Borba mine was exquisite in color and clarity, and all the stones were large. If he could buy just a year's production, he could become the premier emerald dealer in the Southwest. Southwest, *hell*. He could be the emerald king of the United States! He just needed the mine, and curse or not, he'd have it—if this woman would only help him.

He looked to her, still lost in her grief, and spoke kindly, "Listen, *Dona* Isabella, perhaps I can help you. If you would let me, I would gladly help you set up mining operations and market your production."

"Just like that other one helped me, that other *filho-da-mãe* that Itzhak sent? Sorry, *Gringo*, but there's nothing left to steal. He broke in here and stole our map. It was all we had… someone else already took our money."

Jack feigned shock and said, "I don't believe it!" Though knowing Heiner, he knew it could be true.

"Believe it. He came here, polite as can be, just like you, asking the questions you're asking. And I told him the same as I'm going to tell you—I won't help you at all. It's my husband's mine, and as long as there is a chance of his being alive, I won't tell a soul anything of his secrets…" Her face fell as she considered her husband's survival. "But he's not alive. I don't want to believe that, but it's true. It's true, I know it. Why else would he have abandoned us?"

She began to cry again.

"And since I wouldn't tell your friend anything, he broke into our house, the house of a new widow and her poor daughter. He broke in while we were away in town, rifled through all of Joaquim's papers and stole the map that he drew for us before he left for the final time. Now I don't even know where my husband's mine is. I haven't a clue and couldn't tell you if I wanted to—which I don't. He never told me anything, other than he found it in a dangerous place and that he would never be able to file a mining claim on it. He said he would be murdered if he tried."

"That can't be true. In Brazil, any Brazilian has a right to mine for anything, anywhere he finds it. He is obligated to split the profits with the landowner, but it's his right to mine, even if it's in the middle of a working farm or even in the middle of a city."

"You speak Portuguese well enough, young man, but it's obvious you know nothing of Brazil. We have many laws and many rights, but not everyone is obliged to keep the laws. And not everyone's rights are honored. Certain people are above the law and certain people below it. Look at me. Look at where I am and what I have. I have nothing, and because of that, no one, not even the police, will help me.

"I've lost everything—first my sons, then my husband, after he finally found what he was looking for, and now that's lost to us as well. And the money we made from all of those emeralds he sold to Itzhak? It's gone, too. All gone. It disappeared soon after Joaquim did. The police told us that he probably took it and flew to Miami. They say he signed the withdrawal slip. That's a lie, and I know it. I questioned them about it and filed complaint after complaint, but the police chief told me he was gone and that I had better accept it and leave well enough alone. He was not polite. He seemed angry and scared, but whatever or whoever got to him held more power over him than the thought of wronging a widow.

"Somebody murdered poor Joaquim and stole all our money. It was probably the police themselves on orders from above, or it could have been Itzhak for all I know or that awful German that he sent. I never thought Itzhak to be a person who could do something like this, but what do I know? The world's come apart, and I'm a fool. I always have been. I let a dreamer fill my head with stars when I was a girl, and I've been paying for it ever since. Twenty-six years of marriage left me with nothing but mourning for all I've lost—and fear for my daughter's future."

Tears welled in her eyes again.

Jack stayed where he was, not wanting to break the silence as she worked to calm herself. "When I was my daughter's age, I lived in the most beautiful city in the world in a big apartment on its most famous beach. I had a dozen rich boys from good families after me—a dozen to pick from for the future. Well, I picked wrong and look where it got me! And my daughter, my poor Marisa, what does she have? Nothing. I'll never get her out of here and into college, not now. How can I? I have no money. The price of this house wouldn't buy three year's rent in Cuiabá, much less Rio. We lost it all. We fell out of our class, and we will never get back in. It's impossible. We're poor now forever, and there's nothing I can do about it. Marisa will be a peon's wife. There's nothing for her here and no way out."

She shuddered at the thought of the soft skin of her pretty young daughter touched by the rough hands of a muddy gold miner or dusty *peão*, and she began to sob.

After a few moments, she began to regain her composure, but nearly shouted. "Now you get out of here and never come back! We don't need any more help from people like you. I don't want promises, and I've given up on dreaming, so don't bother trying to sell me one. I don't want your promised help. We've had enough. *Chega*! If you want to find the Borba mine, go find your German friend and steal my map from him—he's the one who knows now. But you'd better be careful in your search or you're liable to disappear like my husband did. If I were you, I'd go back to wherever you came from. You're not wanted here, not by me or anybody else, and you had best watch out. Now leave us in peace!"

She slammed the door in his face.

"Wait, *Senhora* Fontes. Please! I can help you. Be reasonable."

He knocked on the door, but his knocks brought nothing but the irritating squawk of the parrot. Dejected, he turned around and walked through the cluttered yard to his car, which he got into and started. As he put the car in gear, he looked back to the dingy little house.

Electricity passed through him at what he saw there: a beautiful young woman was watching him through a window, but she moved back into shadow the moment that he saw her. That instant of sight had made its mark, it confirmed her beauty and left him breathless.

He stared for a few more minutes, but she was lost from view. He sighed and then reluctantly drove back into town, trying to put her out of mind and trying to figure out what he could do next.

Who could lead him to the mine, he wondered? He would have to somehow track down Heiner who was now already a month in the lead. Some things never change, he thought glumly as he bounced his way toward Poconé full of questions and without much hope for a single answer.

Chapter Three

"*Mais um?*" queried the bearded waiter, who in a greasy T-shirt and flip-flops, looked more like a shade-tree mechanic after a day of pulling engines than a person who should be handling food.

"*Por que não?*" answered Jack. *Why not have another one? There's nothing left for me in this town but drink.* The waiter grabbed the large, empty bottle from the dirty table and returned with another—this one sweating in the hot afternoon air almost as much as the grubby man who delivered it. He poured a bit into Jack's empty glass, then moved on to another table where his few other patrons were having churrasco, the Brazilian orgy of salty grilled beef, chicken hearts and sausage.

Jack had been hungry when he entered what was billed as the best restaurant in town, but one look at the beef with rivers of grease dripping from it washed away his appetite. He wanted a beer then, even more than before. The half-liter Antártica now perspiring in his hand was his third in an hour. The others hadn't helped at all. He'd hoped that they would.

The day had not improved since The Professor's wife had slammed the door in his face that morning. On the way back to town, he had a flat at a crossroads that was littered with broken bottles and candle wax. It was a macumba sight: voodoo in Brazil was practiced where roads crossed, and whatever spirit released during the last full moon either didn't like him or his radials. Then to make things worse, when he opened the hatchback to fetch the spare tire, he found it almost flat. He'd had to creep back on the rutted road toward town at about ten miles an hour.

Once back in Poconé, he made a beeline to the local whorehouse, figuring it a mandatory stop for his rival. If anyone remembered Heiner, it would be the social hostesses. He got there at noon but still had to wake everyone up.

The girls looked grim in the afternoon, like vampires caught out in the light. Late night miniskirts and coquettish glances had turned to oversized T-shirts and fish-eyed stares under the scrutiny of day. It took a lot of patience and several *cruzeiros* to wake the girls up from their stupor and to jog their memories, but it was for nothing—none of them had been with anyone but the locals in ages. Foreigners who made it this far from civilization were into eco-tours, not the around-the-world in an hour adventures these girls offered. The more lascivious tourists generally never left the confines of Recife, Salvador or the Zona Sul in Rio. Brazil to them was a bordello by the beach—cheap beer and all-night dancing.

On waking, the drowsy girls warmed to Jack's money and then to him: he was more handsome and less dusty than their average customers, all of whom rode into town in the beds of trucks or on the backs of horses. Yes, Jack looked good to them indeed, but the inverse wasn't true.

Jack had just spent a week in Rio, and pictures of bikinied bodies sashaying along its beaches still burned as visions in his mind. These backwater beauties didn't stand a chance, not at that moment anyway. He backed his way into the street and thought about his sometime friend. Heiner must have found what he was looking for in a hurry if hadn't stopped in for a quickie. These spooky women wouldn't have bothered him a bit. Heiner went tribal in Angola the moment he cleared customs. The German had his appetites, big appetites, but his tastes were simple. He wasn't one to pick out colors when he ate M&Ms. They were all good to him, and he ate them by the handful. Heiner must be hot on the trail if he didn't take time to stop in here, thought Jack sourly. For him, though, the trail was growing colder by the hour.

After he left Poconé's lone pleasure palace, he drove around randomly looking for clues. The town was alive with posters. It was election time in Brazil, and the car radio droned continuous propaganda. Whichever station Jack tuned to shouted forth promises of everything for everybody in incredible, monotonous bombasts. The media was obliged by law to give all candidates free advertising, so for one brief instant in time, samba and *música certeneja* lost their crowns, usurped and banished by the powers that be, and *futebol* fell to politics as the main topic of heated conversation.

Posters were plastered on every vertical surface: walls, windows, telephone poles and also the backs of men. Elections meant logoed T-shirts for the poor, and the candidates clothed the less fortunate with the same gusto they had when they wall-papered cities.

Everywhere he turned as he wound his way through the crooked streets, he was met by the portrait of one candidate or another waving the green, blue and yellow proudly. There were the candidates for the PDT, the PDD, the PT, the PLL, the PSDB—one for every possible combination of letters— and if the poster count was any indication of the will of the people, one man was clearly in the lead. The warm, caring face of *Senador* Afonso Fonseca de Cabral, candidate for the *presidência*, smiled benignly at him from every possible angle everywhere he went. "Fonseca for change. Fonseca for a new Brazil. Fonseca for president!"

Under the senator's gaze he had spent the rest of the afternoon wandering around Poconé continuing his search, talking to grocers, barmen and desk clerks at pousadas, the stark bed and breakfasts that passed for hotels in the interior. He questioned anyone else he could corner. Had they seen or heard of a tall, blond German who liked the ladies? Did they know the whereabouts of Professor Fontes?

The only thing gleaned from all his questions about Heiner was that many foreigners passed through Poconé on their way to birdwatch or fish in the Pantanal, and many could have fit his description. But as to their nationality? No one knew. Gringos were gringos, usually imported from Cuiabá, just images framed in the windows of Volkswagen buses headed south for Pantanal safaris.

Sometimes the odd foreigner did blunder through on his own, stopping in town in a rental car, lost and asking for directions in halting, mangled Portuguese read straight from a brightly colored phrase book. But no one knew anything about the German. He had managed to pass through town like a ghost and had vanished. Who could say where he went?

The answer lay with The Professor, but he was gone too, and nobody seemed willing to tell Jack where he went. All his questions about the man were answered by tight lips that signaled the end of conversation. The people in town knew something, he was sure of that, but nobody was talking. He sensed fear in them all.

He refilled his glass and sipped his beer, staring glumly at the bottle before him and counting out his options, which didn't take long because he didn't have any, not a single one, other than to go back and try to reason with *Senhora* Fontes, who seemed sure to slam the door in his face again. Or he could give up and go back to Rio. What was he to do? Heiner had managed to beat him once again and had taken all clues to the location of the mine with him.

Jack picked up his bottle to pour another glass, but found it empty. He then motioned the grimy waiter to bring another. Poconé had been a dead end, like every other trip he'd made since leaving Africa, where his luck ran out and abandoned him. All this trip had done was cost him money, money that he could scarcely afford to spend. He'd been in South America for almost two months and had absolutely nothing to show for it. He tapped his empty glass on the table, making a flower of little interconnected water stains. *I guess it's back to Africa*, he thought dejectedly. *It's my last chance. I'm sure not getting anywhere by staying here.* He stared down into his beer defeated.

"*Da licença. Senhor Tate?*"

Jack looked up, startled. Standing before him was the girl he had seen in the window as he left the Fontes place. She was beautiful, with bright brown eyes, more golden than brown, the color of hand-rubbed oak. Her hair was the color of night, or of polished obsidian in sunlight, mirror-like and long. Her skin was olive, tanned deep, and her features were fine and well formed: high cheek bones, a thin, perfect nose and full sensuous lips that didn't quite shut, revealing just a hint of white teeth. Hidden in a peasant dress, her form was hard to gauge, but by looking at her lithe, muscled arms, her slender, tendoned neck and the slight brush of her breasts against the cotton, Jack knew that it pleased him. She was gorgeous, but couldn't have been much over twenty.

He stood and held out his hand, "You're Professor Fontes' daughter, aren't you?"

She accepted his hand, shook it and answered, "Yes, I am. My name is Marisa."

"My name's Jack. Glad to meet you. Please, have a seat and join me."

He stepped around the table and pulled out a chair into which she sat.

"Would you like anything to drink? Beer, a soft drink?" he asked.

"Oh, I don't know, Mr. Tate."

"Call me Jack. Please have something. The pleasure's mine."

"All right then, Jack, a Guaraná."

"A Guaraná it is!" He called to the waiter to bring Marisa's drink, Guaraná, the sparkling national soft drink favored by Amazonian Indians since antiquity, and also the beer that he had already requested.

He sat down and looked at the girl across from him. She was gorgeous, unnervingly so. He encountered many beautiful women in his business as an exclusive jeweler and designer. There is truth to the adage that doctors never marry ugly; neither do millionaires. The majority of his clients were head-turners, even most of the older ones, but this girl knocked them all flat. She was almost otherworldly, with an exotic look that surpassed any of the sunbathers that flocked along the strands of Ipanema, Copacabana or Leblon.

She seemed out of time and out of place in the heart of South America, meters from a swamp that was one of the most inhospitable regions on earth. She belonged in dreams. Jack felt a warm flush under her charming gaze, and he felt an intense desire for her that he wasn't sure he liked.

It wasn't the time for such thoughts, so he tried to bury them and turn his mind to business. *Why is she here? What does she want from me? What questions should I ask to draw her out?* All of his practiced small talk and salesmanship had disappeared with her entrance. He was without words.

As she looked across the table at him through the silence that separated them, he wondered if she sensed his discomfort. A woman as beautiful as she would surely know, but she was just barely a woman. Then again, beauties grow up fast.

The waiter came over with their drinks and this gave him a chance at small talk. "Well, here come our drinks!"

The waiter sat them down slowly and took the opportunity to leer at her. "Hello, Marisa," he said. "How are you today?"

"Fine, João. And yourself?" she asked off-handedly, still looking at Jack.

"Good. Good." He stood beside the table smiling, staring lustily down at her, saying nothing and making no attempt to leave.

A customer from the other side of the restaurant hollered for him to bring more meat. He nodded with a scowl, then reluctantly walked away, wiping his moist palms on his belly as he went.

"You eat here?"

"No, not really. Sometimes with my parents, but this is a small town, so everybody knows everybody else."

"I guess they would. You must be very popular here with all the boys, being as pretty as you are."

She frowned. "No again. Not really. They would like me to be popular with them, but I'm not interested. I have plans for my life, and they don't include any cowhands or panners from Poconé."

"What are your plans?" asked Jack, taken aback by the will in her words and the iron in her voice.

"I'm going to Rio and I will live like my mother did when she was young. I'm going to live in a nice apartment by the beach and wear nice dresses, and I am going to meet nice, interesting people. I will go there first to study at the university where my father taught, and then I will go into business, maybe with my father. I have thought a lot about becoming a jeweler. I've been around gold mines all my life. I know all about it, and I know all about gemstones, too. My father is a geologist, and ever since we were kids, he would teach us about precious stones. We knew our minerals before we knew the alphabet. He would show us samples every day, and we would have to tell him what they were. I could recognize all of the Brazilian gems before I was five." She paused, looking thoughtful.

"Are you a geologist?" she asked.

"No, I'm a gemologist—that's a person who identifies and evaluates gemstones."

"I know what a gemologist is! You think I didn't know?" Her eyes narrowed at the perceived offense.

"No, not at all, Marisa. It's just that most people outside of the jewelry industry don't. They think gemology is something like astrology or palmistry. When I tell them I'm a gemologist, they ask me who's going to win the next world series. It's not a very common occupation. I started studying it when I became a gem buyer. It really pays to know what you're looking at these days. All that glitters certainly isn't gold, or diamond or emerald for that matter. There's synthetic everything today, and the trade is full of crooks who will sell you synthetics as naturals in a second if you're not watching. When I first got into this business, I trusted the wrong people and got burned. Now I don't have to trust anyone. With a few simple tests, I can verify whether or not a stone is real and if it's natural, not synthetic. By testing a stone here and there, I keep my suppliers honest, and I save myself a lot of money."

"Are you rich? My parents were wealthy before I was born. They lived on the beach in Leblon. That was a long time ago. *Papai* will make us rich again. He already has, but somebody stole our money."

"Yes, I heard about that. Sorry. No, I'm not rich. I would like to be one day..." Jack was struck by the fact that she talked of her father in the present tense. "Wait a second—Marisa, you talk as if your father is alive, but your mother told me that he and your brothers are dead."

"My brothers are dead," she said sadly. "They died four years ago in a mining accident at the end of the dry season. We were setting up to work one of our gold claims in a dried river bottom, bolting up flumes and rolling out hoses, getting ready for the rains that would give us the water we needed to mine. My brothers were in the river bottom, surveying the clay and positioning suction hoses, and my father and I were getting our portable generator set up when it happened..."

She stopped talking. Remembering still hurt.

Jack felt her pain, and it galled him to hurt her more by asking her to continue—her pretty sadness wrenched his heart—but he needed to know.

"What happened, Marisa?"

"A flash flood. Sometimes we have them here. These rivers are fed from the mountains north of Cuiabá. Sometimes if it rains hard in the mountains, we get flooded. That day was one of the worst in anyone's memory. A wall of water came roaring down the river bottom and washed my brothers away. There was nothing we could do. Once the water hit them, we never saw them again. We searched for days, but never found anything. They must have been washed down into the Rio Paraguay. We never found any trace of them after the water went down, but we didn't really expect to. Nothing survives in the rivers here at the end of the dry season—too many hungry *piranhas* and caimans."

She stopped talking and looked down to the table. Tears filled her eyes, but she didn't cry. Jack placed a hand on hers and patted it.

"I'm sorry to hear about that, Marisa. I didn't know. Itzhak Blum told me of your brothers—from when he knew them in Rio, when they were just boys. He said that they would grow up to be real lady-killers."

She brightened at the comment, then smiled and looked up.

"They were, Jack. They were. Every girl in Poconé wanted my brothers and many got them, for a while, anyway."

She laughed.

"If the river hadn't taken my brothers, someone's father probably would have, but they were good brothers, Jack. They took such good care of me. It's been four years this month, but it seems like yesterday. I miss them."

A tear flowed then, and Jack handed her a napkin.

"Thank you. I'll be all right in just a moment."

She brought herself back under control quickly and seemed embarrassed for breaking down. Jack needed to ask her about her father, but she answered the question before he had to ask.

"I don't believe that my father's dead, Jack. I just can't believe it. He is a strong man, bigger than life, absolutely fearless, and he knows what he is doing. He knows this country better than anybody, and he knows mines. too. My father is very careful and very serious when he works. The only mistake he ever made in life was letting my brothers work in that river bottom at the beginning of the floods, but how was he supposed to know? No, I think *Papai's* alive. Maybe he's hurt or is in trouble, but I won't ever believe he's dead until I see his body. We need to go find him and get him out of whatever trouble he's in."

Jack looked at her and wondered whether her confidence in her father's survival was just the irrational hope of the bereaved or if she knew something he didn't. Death was a touchy subject, but he needed answers.

"I don't mean to cause you any more pain," he said. "But I have to ask certain questions..."

"You don't think my father's alive, do you?"

"I'd like to think so. I came here to find him, but I'm a bit confused. Your mother said the police told her that he took your family's money and ran away, but she seems certain that he's dead. You think that he's alive, and no one else in this town will even talk to me about him. I really don't know what to think."

"*Mamãe* always thinks the worst. Life hasn't been easy on her. She left a perfect life in Rio to follow my father in his search of his dreams, and she never had a chance to get it back. Now after the death of my brothers, she's pretty much given up on everything. She lost hope and just doesn't care. She never even leaves the house anymore. All she does is sit in the dark, looking at pictures and talking to Eduardo, our parrot, about her youth. You know when *Papai*, finally brought home the emeralds he had promised her, she barely looked at them and didn't say a word. They came too late. *Mamãe's* losing her mind, and I need to get her out of here to help her get it back. If you help me find my father and do what you told my mom you'd do for us—buy

39

our emeralds—we'll be able to go to Rio and do everything we ever wanted."

"But wait a minute. Your mother said she doesn't have any emeralds."

"That's right—we don't, only the one my father gave to her to celebrate the find."

"Well then, where are you going to get the emeralds?"

"From the Borba mine, of course."

"From the mine?" Jack questioned loudly.

Marisa leaned over quick and said sharply, "Keep your voice down!"

"Sorry," he whispered. "You have a copy of the map? Your mother said Heiner stole it."

"Yes, he did, and I do have a copy."

"Where?"

"Right here." She smiled and pointed to her temple.

"You memorized it?" Jack looked incredulous.

"I didn't need to memorize it, Jack. I've been there—twice. I was with my father when he found it. He always took us mining whenever we weren't in school. I was swinging a pick as soon as I could lift one. Mining has always been a family thing with us, with *Papai* and us kids anyway, sort of like baseball for you Americans. And the Borba mine was our family legend. My brothers and I were as obsessed with it as our father was.

The last time we saw *Papai*, he was headed back to the mine. He was going to make one last run for emeralds before we moved to Rio, so if he's alive, that's where we'll find him. I have to find him. I have to know, Jack, and whether he's alive or not, I need to dig out enough crystals to give me and *Mamãe* a new start. I would have gone looking for him a month ago, but didn't want to risk going on my own. It can be dangerous in the Pantanal, and one should never travel alone. Unfortunately, there is no one around here I trust to take with me. I couldn't take *Mamãe*. She's too far gone and too old. There's really no one else to ask but you. Will you go with me? The mine is ours, but we will sell you everything you want at a fair price."

"Of course, I'll go with you. We can leave right now. My car's outside."

"No, not by car. Things are never that easy. We'll need horses to get there, three horses. One for each of us and one for *Papai*, and we'll need food, water and some equipment."

"Sure, Marisa, anything you want. But there are too many unanswered questions. The first one is, why all the secrecy? Why don't you file a claim for your mining rights— you don't have to own the land or even have the landowner's permission to mine in Brazil. You must know that. Why don't you file your claim with the state, and then have the police or the fire department go out with you to search for your father?"

"I know all about mining law, Jack, but in this part of Brazil, the laws don't apply, not to everybody. The man who owns the land where our mine is located is very powerful. If we made our mine known and tried to file a claim for it, I'm sure the claim would magically be transferred to him one way or another before the courthouse closed its doors that day."

"Who could be powerful enough to do that? Even if a person were well connected, surely you could fight them in court."

"Believe me, Jack, if we started a fight with him, it would never get to court."

"Who is this person?"

"If I tell you, maybe it would change your mind about helping me."

41

"No, I want to know, but it really doesn't matter. I need those emeralds as much as you do. I'd help you get them even if they were in the Tower of London. But who is it?"

"He's right behind you."

"What?" Jack swung around to face yet another pasted-up portrait of the leading presidential candidate, the populist Senator Afonso Fonseca de Cabral, leering down at him with the inflated compassion of a drunken father, misty in his cup on his daughter's sixteenth birthday.

Fonseca for the people. Fonseca for a new Brazil. Fonseca the landlord who had the locals too scared to answer simple questions. Jack swallowed. The stakes had risen in the game, and he wasn't sure he had the ante. He didn't need to ask his second question; the answer was obvious—she was asking him to help her because only a foreigner would be dumb enough to try.

Jack felt the dirty walls of the restaurant closing-in on him. But it was too late to stop. He was as drawn to the legendary Borba mine as her father had been, as much as Chico Borba himself, but not out of historical obsession or the hope of fame or anything else like that. He simply needed the emeralds very badly. He hoped that Lady Luck was shining down on him, but he didn't feel her. Even the beauty of Marisa sitting across the table did nothing to stir him. He was too numb. He could hear the metallic ring of doors swinging shut in his African prison, and he could hear the boots of his inquisitors pounding in the dust.

"Are you okay, Jack?" questioned Marisa, worry on her brow.

"What? Oh, sure. Sure." He filled his glass with beer, downed it. He looked to her, smiled blankly and asked, "When do you want to start out?"

Chapter Four

"**A**re you sure these horses are going to make it?" Jack questioned loudly. Marisa was in the lead, her packhorse plodding assuredly on the trail.

She turned her head to answer, sounding miffed. "I told you they would be fine. These are *Pantaneira* horses. They are tough! You'll see."

Jack looked down doubtfully at his mount. Its head swaggered back and forth as it walked forward through the brush, and he felt that at any moment it might give up its spirit and topple to the ground, pinning him down when it did. He watched its sharp withers play beneath its loose hide; it looked as though its bones might saw through the surface at any minute.

"These are the skinniest horses I have ever seen. Do you really think it's safe to ride them into the Pantanal? What happens if they die? What would we do then?"

Marisa reined to a stop and twisted around in her saddle. The extra packhorse, meant for her father, had been trailing her on a loosely hung lead rope and came to a placid stop.

"Look, Jack, these are the best horses I could get. All the horses are skinny here at the end of the dry season. They feed on grasses, and there aren't many left this time of the year, so they're lean. But they're used to it. They can take it; believe me. They'll be fine."

She looked to the gringo behind her, already bathed in sweat before eight in the morning. Then she smiled and added, "I'll bet they have more staying power than you do!"

She laughed, turned around and kicked her mount softly forward.

Jack followed her, still doubtful, but silent.

The hours passed with the rising sun, and gradually the scenery changed from ordered soybean and sunflower fields to low-lying scrub thicket crowned with scattered date palms, blooming pink *piuva* trees, and scarlet *pau-de-novatos*.

They had set out from Poconé before dawn. Jack had spent the day before running around town trying to get all of the provisions that Marisa had listed, but couldn't get everything locally. In fact, he couldn't find much of anything. Poconé was not an outfitter's Mecca.

He'd been forced to drive all the way back to Cuiabá to finish shopping, and still it wasn't easy. He'd driven across that city in a rush, scrambling from store to store trying to get supplies before they closed. Eventually he did manage to find almost everything they needed—a pick, two shovels, kerosene lanterns, an ax, two hammocks, a rifle, dried beans, dried meat, a small tent, first aid supplies, bug repellent, blankets, water purifying tablets, and all of the other things people need when they walk away from man's habitations and step into the wild. This wasn't a weekend outing in Yosemite. Here there were no forest rangers. Trouble meant trouble in the Pantanal, no helicopter rescues, no hospitals, and no concern or helping hands. It was as wild as the world could get, and in it you were on your own.

It was night by the time he'd finished buying their supplies, and it was near midnight when he reached his seedy *posada* in Poconé. Sleep took him before he hit the pillow, if sleep took him at all. It seemed that his alarm clock chirped the second his eyes closed—3:30 a.m., time to drive out to the Fontes place to meet Marisa, who was to be ready with the horses for their journey.

Now he was tired, saddle-sore, hungry, thirsty, and very nearly baking in the heat. He looked at his watch—11 a.m. They'd been on horseback for nearly seven hours and still the horses plodded on, with Marisa's horse and the packhorse in the lead. She rode straight-backed and lovely, swaying with the movement of her horse, looking happy and at home. He'd sweat through his shirt hours before, but it was now dry—he had nothing left to sweat.

She rode on, as fresh as any orchid they passed along the way. He accepted his discomfort and grimly followed atop his horse. He wouldn't be the one to ask for a break. It had to be her. It came three hours later, when they encountered a pond where they could water the horses.

"Why don't we take a break, Jack? It's been a long ride and we should rest the horses."

He could have sung a psalm of thanks if his throat hadn't been so parched, so he answered simply, "Well, okay, if you think we should."

"Why don't we then?"

She dismounted and led her horse and the pack horse down to water. As they approached the pond, the bank became alive with caimans which, startled awake, splashed into the water.

"Jesus, Marisa, get back! It's full of caimans!" He grabbed her arm and yanked her back.

She laughed and pulled herself free. "Take it easy. Haven't you ever seen a caiman before?"

"Sure I have, in the zoo behind bars where they belong. And I've seen crocodiles too, in Africa, and nobody was fool enough to get near them there either!"

"The *jacaré* here don't bother you, Jack. I've been swimming in rivers with them all of my life. They won't bite you unless you step on them. Then it's bad news, because they bite and roll you under, out of reflex. But normally they just lie there. The only dangerous *jacaré* is a nesting mother. They are the ones to watch for, but these here," she pointed toward the barely visible eyes that watched them from a few yards away in the pond. "They have more to fear from you. They taste better to us than we do to them, so people kill them by the thousands."

"You like caiman?"

"Oh yes, the tail meat is delicious! But we don't eat them anymore, not my family anyway. There aren't that many left—too much poaching. The skin traders kill them and smuggle the skins out through Paraguay. The sad thing is that they don't even bother with the meat. They just leave it on the ground to rot."

"But, Marisa, what do you mean there aren't many left. This pond's crawling with the things."

"That's because it's the dry season. After the rains stop, the rivers go down, and the caimans that don't make it to the rivers get stuck in these ponds, or they dig a little pond for themselves. They're all grouped together now, but once the floods come, you hardly ever see one until the rains come again.

"It wasn't like that when I was a girl. They used to be plentiful, and we'd eat them all the time. Not anymore. *Papai* forbids it, now that they're in danger."

Jack looked out at the dozen pairs of eyes watching him from the water. All of Marisa's assurances hadn't yet convinced him of the harmlessness of the toothy reptiles. His adrenaline was still pumping from hearing the gators splash into the water. He was ready to run, but neither

Marisa nor the horses paid them much attention. She led her horses to the bank where they began to drink. Jack followed her with his, still ready to fly in a second if one of the beasts should swim his way.

While the horses drank, they passed a water bottle between them. They brought as many 2-liter, plastic soda bottles full of water as they thought the horses could carry, but it wouldn't last long. Marisa told him that they would have to drink river water in a few days. He eyed the muddy water of the caiman pond with disgust, wondering how many strains of exotic and still unclassified bacteria swam in it, and if its murky color was due to the local soil or to caiman shit.

Jack looked out again to the eyes that were still watching them. They just sat there, immobile, a bunch of saurian couch potatoes—they didn't look like much at all. He felt masculine stirrings and had the notion that he would like to kill one of them, right there in front of Marisa, where he could serve up its tail on a plate and carve her some shoes from its leather… or maybe even a G-string. He looked over to her. He could see her drinking from the bottle tilted up in her hands. Her cheeks sucked in and her throat undulated as she swallowed the warm water in long, draining gulps. He felt primal with her out in the wild, in the heart of South America. His blood pulsed with being a man.

"You know, I think I'd like to hunt an caiman, Marisa. Just to do it. Just to know that I could…"

He stared back into the pond, feeling strong and somewhat ferocious.

Marisa looked out to the *jacaré* that he was eyeing and said thoughtfully, "Well there's really not much to it, Jack. All you have to do is shoot them between the eyes or whack them in the head with a hammer. Getting them in the boat once they're dead is the hard part. The big ones weigh a ton."

She paused for a moment, watching the water thoughtfully. "Why don't we have lunch. Let's go sit in the shade of that *piuva* over there."

She led her horses away to the welcoming shade of the big, pink-blossomed tree and left Jack by the water's edge, deflated.

Jack stood there a minute, wondering what had gotten into him. He'd hunted with his father as a child and remembered bagging his first and only deer, just after his fifteenth birthday. His father's pride in him had been enormous, but he didn't feel proud at all as he trudged through the brush with the weight of the deer slung across his shoulders, its glazed eye staring dully at him for the hour it took to get back to the truck. He had never really enjoyed hunting and wondered what was going on with him now.

Maybe it was the wilderness, knowing that they were truly on their own. Or maybe it was the girl. Marisa was gorgeous enough to bring the animal out of any man, but she was way too young for him. Besides, they were looking for her father, who was probably dead, and her mother was as nutty as a fruitcake. No, now wasn't the time for romance for her. *Shake it off Jack*, he told himself angrily. *You're almost old enough to be her dad*. He was just sunbaked, that's all. That's what it was. He chuckled at his silliness with the caimans, then walked over to the shade where she was laying out a picnic on a blanket.

"What's for lunch, *garota*?"

She smiled at the appellation, which meant "little girl."

"I bought some fresh food for today and tomorrow with the money you gave me. We feast today, but pretty soon it will just be sun-dried beef, rice and the beans. But for now, it's ham and cheese sandwiches. Look, I even brought mustard." She beamed at him as she held up the jar.

Jack didn't have the heart to tell her he hated mustard, so he smiled as he accepted the thick sandwich, its inner crust already dripping yellow.

"Thanks," he said.

"Where are you from?" she asked, after swallowing her first bite.

"The United States."

"I knew that! You have an accent. I mean where in the U.S."

"I live in Houston, Texas."

"Texas. It's full of cowboys, just like around here. I've seen it in the movies."

"Well, maybe in some parts of Texas, but not in Houston. The cowboys we have just sit around in bars drinking beer. I bet there's not one in a hundred who have even ridden a horse."

"You don't seem too sure of yourself on a horse either, Jack."

"I would hardly call that a horse."

He looked over to his pitiful mount. He had taken off its saddle before he sat down, so now he had a full view of its swayed back. Its ribs stuck out like mainsail battens and its knobby, spindled legs somehow held it up as it munched on a palm frond, clearly unconcerned with his appraisal.

"Call him what you want, Jack, but you've got to admit that he's a worker. These *Pantaneira* horses may not be much to look at, but they're tough. They'll carry you 'til they drop," she said proudly.

"That's what I'm afraid of," he replied.

They finished their sandwiches, then ate a few oranges for dessert. The acidic sweetness of the oranges tasted good in the heat.

As they were eating, Marisa continued with her questions.

"So is Houston a big city?"

"Yes, it is. It's either the third or fourth largest in America, I'm not sure which."

"So, it's as big as Cuiabá?"

Jack almost laughed at the comparison of the Brazilian frontier boomtown to the city where he lived.

"It might be even bigger," he responded.

Her eyes grew with the thought.

"Is it a beach city like Rio?"

"No, Marisa, it's not. We have beaches in Galveston, about fifty miles—ninety kilometers—from the city, but they certainly don't stand up to Leblon or Barra. The water is brownish, and the people aren't the same. I can't quite explain it, but something about Rio makes it special. It's not just the mountains and forest that surround the city and reach down to the beach. It's something more. I think that it's the Cariocas, the people of Rio, who make their city unique. There is a sensuousness in them that sets them apart from anybody else I can think of."

She pulled off a slice of orange and slid it in her mouth while she pondered the clouds and thought of Rio.

"My mother loves her city so much. I hope I can take her back soon... I wonder if I will fit in there? All my life I've lived here in a swamp. I wonder if I'd do well in Rio?"

Jack watched her eat the orange and pictured her walking along the Avenida Atlântica in "dental floss," a Brazilian string bikini.

He answered her with all the truth inside him, "I'm sure you would do very well in Rio, Marisa. Very well, indeed. And once we find your father and his emeralds, I would be more than happy to show you around the city myself."

"Thanks, Jack. That's very nice of you. Is that a promise then?"

He smiled. "It sure is."

She smiled back, then stood and checked the angle of the sun. "It must be close to three."

Jack checked his watch, which read 3:10 p.m.

"We should be going," she said. "It gets dark around seven, so we can ride for another three hours and still have an hour of daylight to set up camp. Let's go."

They saddled their horses and went on their way, Marisa in front, leading the pack horse, and Jack following. As they rode along, he watched her swaying in the saddle in her jeans, her back outlined in sweat through her buff cotton shirt, and he couldn't stop thinking about her on a beach. He sighed. It was going to be a long trip.

Chapter Five

As they rode the final miles to the mine, Jack thought back over the past eleven days, which had been some of the most interesting, harrowing and confusing days of his life. He recalled his first night in the Pantanal, when they were setting up camp after an endless day of plodding through the bush and burning heat.

Marisa picked a spot near a small creek, a cluster of trees on a low hummock that would become an island, she told him, once the rains came. She busied herself by setting the horses loose to graze, slinging her hammock and collecting kindling for a cooking fire. Jack asked her if she needed any help, but she said no. She wanted him to rest and let her do the cooking. Exhausted as he was from their grueling first day, he didn't argue and did as he was told. He quickly found two trees, beautiful in flower and full of red berries, to which he tied his hammock. Sleep took him as soon as he climbed in.

Jack awoke to a burning on his face and neck.

"Aghh! Aghh!"

He slapped at the pain, rolled out of the hammock and fell to the ground.

"Aghh!"

He was on fire.

"Aghh!"

Marisa looked up from her cooking to see him stagger to his feet and brush at his face with both hands.

"What's wrong?" she asked as she ran to him, alarmed.

"Ants. I've got ants all over me. She saw them then, crawling on his face, in his hair and down the collar of his shirt onto his chest and back. She immediately started unbuttoning his shirt.

"What are you doing?" he asked, as he hopped around her and batted at the army of ants that swarmed him.

"They're in your clothes. You have to get undressed."

She pulled his shirt free and started pelting him with it to knock away the ants.

"Take off your pants, Jack. They're all over you."

It was humiliating, but he did as she asked and quickly kicked off his boots and struggled out of his Levi's. She picked them up and began swatting at him. With the heavy denim, she soon had his attackers on the run. When all the ants were gone, she stepped back and looked at him as he stood there in his white boxers, which were comical to her, as Brazilians believe in brevity of briefs. He was covered with dozens of tiny welts.

"How in the world did you get so many ants on you, Jack?"

"I don't know!" he replied, scratching himself fiercely. "All I did was lie down and take a nap. The next thing I knew, they were all over me."

"What did you do, lie down on an ant hill?"

"No, I did not! I was in my hammock, peacefully trying to sleep when they attacked me."

She looked over to his hammock and started choking on laughter that shook her so hard she slapped her thighs to get it out.

"What is it?" he asked, peeved with her laughter at his misery.

"What's so funny?"

"*Ave Maria*, Jack. *Ave Maria*! Why on earth did you tie your hammock to a couple of pau-de-novatos?"

"Novice trees, like greenhorn trees?" he asked.

She nodded in affirmation.

"I don't know. They were the right distance apart. Why? What's wrong with that?"

She looked to his hammock and started laughing again.

"I'm sorry. I'm sorry, really."

She brought herself under control and put on a straight face, but she couldn't hold it and started laughing again.

"I should have thought to warn you about them. I just didn't think about it. Everybody here in the Pantanal knows not to get under a novice tree—they're always full of ants, and if you shake them, the ants will fall all over you."

She looked at him and chuckled harder.

"They bit you all over. You look like a strawberry!"

He was getting angry at the stings and at her laughter, but her glee broke him down and soon he was laughing, too. Laughing and scratching. They laughed together, and he scratched the evening away.

He chuckled at the memory—the welts had disappeared by then, so it was truly funny. He thought back over the days that followed his initiation to the wetlands. As they moved deeper into the Pantanal and encountered more ponds and creeks, they had seen birds by the thousands, by the tens of thousands, maybe by the millions. They witnessed huge flocks of egrets and herons—long-legged great egrets, snowy egrets with their downy tufts, capped egrets, cowbirds, white-necked herons, black-crowned night herons, maguaris, little blue herons, striated herons and tiger herons with their russet caps and mottled feathers. They saw kingfishers, cormorants, cranes and anhingas. They saw ibises, gulls, terns, spoonbills and limpkins, and everywhere they looked were hawks: brown and yellow roadside hawks, gray and leggy crane hawks, mottled savanna hawks, and immense and stately harpy eagles.

Many of the hawks, such as the red-eyed, sharp-beaked snail kites and the large, black-collared hawks, would let them approach within ten feet, totally without fear or simply without interest. Marisa explained that they were fishing birds that would sit on low branches for hours, watching for movement in the water. Then, in an instant, they would dive and swoop low, dab a claw in the water and almost always fly away with a fish.

Lone toucans flapped overhead, following the rainbow of their beaks in a never-ending search for gold, and parakeets and parrots gamboled in the air in green, discordant flights of hundreds. One time, a flock of twenty hyacinth macaws passed above them—enormous parrots, the world's largest, ranging the sky in a syncopated flight of stately blue and yellow. Back and forth, back and forth they went in a raucous, squawking symphony of song and color that seemed predicated on the freedom of flight and the joy of living.

The most magnificent birds they saw were the storks. If storks were truly bearers of good fortune, then the Pantanal must certainly have been the luckiest place on the planet. It teemed with them by the thousands. Colonies of tall and stately black-fringed wood storks crowded in treetop roosts like bouquets of blooming flowers plucked fresh from a giant's garden.

But of all the storks and of all the birds, the Jaburu was the undisputed king.

The Jaburu stork stood four-feet tall atop its spindled legs, a huge white bird with a thick black and scarlet throat, and a long, pointed beak used for spearing fish or, when angered, snapping like castanets. These birds were master fishers, but on occasion they dined on baby caimans and even the odd young anaconda. During the afternoon heat, they powered their wings with an audible *whoosh, whoosh, whoosh* like a helicopter on takeoff. Then they hopped into flight and circled with the thermals until they gracefully disappeared into the altitude.

Jack remembered fondly how Marisa would identify all the creatures by their lyrical Portuguese names. A great kiskadee was a *Bem-te-vi*—a good to see you. An orange-backed oriole was a *João-pinto*—a baby chicken Joe. And an ovenbird was a *João-de-barro*—a muddy Joe. And there were several Marias—*Maria-faceira,* the whistling heron, was an easy Maria to her. But his favorite of them all was the little pied water tyrant known to Brazilians as the *Lavadeira-de-cara-branca*—the white-faced washer woman.

As they traveled along that week, Jack became more and more stricken with Marisa. The moment he met her, he knew her haunting presence wouldn't soon leave him.

A woman with her looks was both a blessing and a curse to the men she brushed into as she waltzed her way through life. Her image would burn a place in memory that couldn't be discarded from any head she turned. Salvation often lay in the tired, yet tried and often true, maxim that beauty and brains don't mix, but Jack was sadly finding that she was an exception to this and about every other rule he knew—sadly because she aroused a passion in him as deep as the guilt he felt for feeling it.

She was twenty-two, just a girl, with a father probably dead and a mother half-insane, while he was thirty-eight, from a different country and culture seven thousand miles away, with a life and lifestyle he didn't want to abandon. Yet, those long days of sweating through the brush on his sway-backed nag, following along, watching her swing in the saddle as the sunlight danced in her hair, stopping at night to sit and tell stories—his about a great wide world full of cities built of glass and steel, and hers about mining and life in the wild. Those long days made him wish for her, and want her, more than anything he knew.

As they would recount the day's adventures—misadventures really, mostly his—they would laugh deeply from the belly, and they would like each other, truly. But those days were almost over. He wished they would never end, but they were ending.

They were almost at the mine, and soon it would be business. They would have to find her father or find out what had happened to him. Dead or alive, Jack didn't relish meeting The Professor, not then. If he was alive, he would certainly quash any chance Jack had of realizing the fantasies that plagued him, the dreams he'd built like mansions in the sky—mansions filled with the sight and smell and smiles and laughter of the woman that he feared to love, this girl too young. Why couldn't he be more like Heiner? If Heiner were in his place, he knew the German would either be smiling in his saddle or nursing a sore, slapped cheek. A slap was what he hoped for Heiner. He was jealous at the thought of the German near her. As he rode on, he sighed, envying the German's lack of scruples and wishing away his own.

Jack tried to shake this melancholy and thought back through the memorable week that had passed. It had been their third night in the bush when Marisa, cooking rice on the fire, had asked him fetch their supply of jerked beef out of the saddlebags. It was then that he learned the true nature of caracaras.

Since the beginning of the trip, he'd enjoyed the company of the strange, yellow-faced eagles with tufts of brown feathers atop their heads that looked like toupees blown loose by the breeze. A half-dozen would always swoop into camp and spend the night at the edge of firelight, jumping around like birds practicing the bunny-hop.

He thought them comical, so he gave them no thought as he sorted through his saddlebags. He had found the beef and started walking over to the fire when he remembered he had forgotten the salt and pepper. He set the heavy bag of meat on the ground and turned back to look through his bags. The shakers had worked their way to the bottom and weren't readily apparent, so he had to dig through his gear and feel for their shape. Intense in his task, he didn't hear the commotion going on behind him until it was too late. When he had the shakers in hand, he pulled them out and turned around to see more than a dozen caracaras ripping through their only supply of meat. He ran to chase them off, but the distance between them was too great. As he approached, the eagles casually lifted off with raucous caws of glee, each carrying a man-sized portion of the rations. They left nothing, except the shreds of what was once a plastic bag.

Jack was devastated. Again, in the Pantanal, he had proven himself a fool, a tenderfoot in a land that fed on them. Feeling like an idiot, he steeled himself to break the news to Marisa—they were in the wilderness without protein and little chance of getting more. His solemn apology was met with laughter.

"You let the caracaras get our meat? Weren't you watching?" asked Marisa, as she looked at the handsome man she liked and respected for his worldliness, but who seemed to bumble through life like a toddler.

"Sorry, Marisa. I never thought that birds would dare try something like that with people around."

"Oh, the caracaras will. We've had them fly in the house and try to steal the food right off our dinner plates. They eat anything, alive or dead; it doesn't matter. They'd peck your eyes out if you gave them the chance. Better be careful, Jack. The way you operate, I might have to buy you some sunglasses and a cane."

She laughed, but he couldn't. Not after what he'd done. What were they going to do?

Without the beef they had nothing but rice and a few days' worth of dried beans. It wasn't nearly enough to last the trip to the mine, much less the trip back. He didn't think the beans would last three days.

"I'm sorry, Marisa. I was careless. It's my fault. Now we don't have enough food to last us the trip," he said, depressed. "I don't know what to tell you. I guess we'll have to go back. I don't know what else to do."

"I do. Let's go fishing."

"Fishing? With what?"

"Oh, I don't know, Jack. I usually use fishing line."

"You have fishing line?"

"I don't know anyone who enters the Pantanal without it. Listen, the rice is done, and we have another hour before sunset, so let's go catch ourselves a fish."

She walked to her gear and quickly found two Coke bottles wrapped with fishing line, both with hook and sinker. With her eyes to the trees, she walked around, searching until she found what she was looking for—berries. With an expert toss of a stick, she rained berries down to earth. Then she gathered them up and offered a handful to Jack.

"What's this?" he asked. "Dessert?"

"No. Bait."

He looked down doubtfully at the little purple inga berries. "You've got to be kidding. Fish don't eat berries. Here, give me one of those lines. I'll show you how to catch a fish."

She handed him a line, then walked down to the river. He followed her slowly, stopping along the way to catch a pocketful of grasshoppers. When he made the riverbank, she was already seated in the sand, leaning back idly with an eye upon her line, not thirty feet from a sleeping caiman.

"Now watch this, *garota*," he said. "This is how to catch a fish."

Jack slid his hook into the thorax of a grasshopper where the back met the head, then jogged it into the river. It barely hit the water before he felt a tug upon his line. He jerked with a smile of triumph, but the hook came up shining and cleaned. "Jesus, Marisa, this river must be full of fish. My hook wasn't in the water for a second."

She didn't answer, and concentrated on her line.

He hooked another hopper and tossed it in—same story, something hit it as soon as it touched the water. Another try brought the same result. Finally, on the fourth attempt, he was faster than the fish and hooked it, tugging it up from the water. The silver, red and yellow of a piranha flashed in the air.

He drew-in the line and palmed the fish.

"Be careful, Jack," called Marisa from her perch a few feet away. "They bite."

Jack looked down at the small fish in his palm. He knew what it was because of the sharp teeth protruding from the mouth of an otherwise innocuous fish. It had the size and look of a Texas blue gill, nothing much to worry about. He looked over to her and smiled.

"You see that? You don't catch fish with berries. They bite on grasshoppers."

His fingers expertly held the fish and moved to pull the hook, but he didn't count on the power of the tough little fish as it swam in the hand that held it and somehow managed to dart up to bite the other hand that worked the hook.

"Aghh," shouted Jack as blood streamed from between his thumb and first finger.

Marisa jumped up from her seat and ran over to him.

"I told you to be careful. They bite!" she said. "Poor man, I'm sorry. I shouldn't have let you touch it. I should have known better."

She led him back to camp, found their medical kit and quickly bandaged his hand, which thumped with the swelling wound. "You've got to learn to listen, Jack. I've lived here all my life, and I know about things here. The only thing you can catch in the dry season with grasshoppers or meat is piranhas, and they're too bony to eat. They make a good soup, but we don't have time to cook it."

She looked down at the bandages.

"That will have to do," she said. "You really need stitches, but you'll be all right if you don't use it too much and let it scab. Now let's catch our dinner before dark."

They walked down to the riverbank where she had been fishing. Her line was still wedged in the stump where she left it, but where it had been slack, it was now taut. She picked it up and pulled hard to bring in a fish.

"Now, look at this, Jack. This is what a berry can catch."

She held up a round, meaty pacu which easily weighed four pounds.

"They love inga berries. Come on, let's go back to camp, and I'll cook us up a dinner. How's your hand?"

He looked from the large fish flapping in the air as she held it by the line back to his hand, which was aching more by the minute. He felt like a fool for the second time in less than an hour.

"I'm fine," he grumbled. "Just fine. I guess I'll try berries next time."

She laughed and carried the fish back to camp where she cleaned it and cooked it quickly.

He smiled at the memory and looked down at the circular scar on the fleshy part of his hand, which was finally beginning to scab properly. He thought it funny that the injury had occurred just six days ago. It seemed a lifetime.

Six days on a horse in a dried-out swamp a thousand miles from anywhere, sleeping in open spaces alive with predators that were dangerous to man. Six days alone with a beautiful woman.

Woman? No. Six days alone with a girl nearly half his age, whom he considered the most attractive he'd ever seen in his life. She moved through the wetlands with the cheerful unconcern of a child sent down the street to fetch a carton of milk, knowing that she can keep the change.

He watched her up ahead, leading him closer and closer to the mine with every passing tree, and leading him closer to realizing his lifetime dream—to finally strike it rich, to find stones that would not only save him, but establish him as a force in the industry.

Force? *Hell*, he'd be a legend if could exploit the Borba mine.

A bag full of emeralds like the one in Itzhak's office would change his life, he was certain. And if he could get a monopoly on the output of the Borba mine? Wealthy customers would seek him out on reputation alone from then on.

But none of that seemed to matter as he followed Marisa up the trail. He watched her, swaying in the saddle, and he wished the trail would never end. He thought back on their many conversations.

"What is your favorite place on earth, Jack?" Marisa asked. They sat by the campfire eating sweet guava and drinking flame-brewed coffee after feasting on a pintado, a large blue, spotted catfish of the region.

"That's a tough question," he answered thoughtfully. "I guess it depends on what you want to do. I like Brussels and Antwerp—I used to go there a lot on business. They are very old and beautiful, most of the buildings there are twice as old as my country.

"I like the beaches in Haifa, Israel, too. The Israelis are a pretty solemn crowd most of the time—I guess anybody would be if they had been at war for their entire history—but they do know how to have fun, and Haifa's certainly fun. Thailand's magnificent along the coast, but Bangkok's a big and dirty nightmare, too much traffic. I like South Africa, not Johannesburg so much, but Durban's a great beach town. Cape Town's nice, too. It's very pretty with lots of colonial charm bunched up by the sea beneath Table Mountain. It's gorgeous. But South Africa lost its charm for me because of its social problems—too much injustice and too much violence. I hope they can get their act together, but I'm not too sure about it. Sub-Saharan Africa hasn't had a very good political track record since the end of colonial rule. I always thought South Africa was the best-run country on the continent, and look how screwed up they were. I just hope they can pull off democracy and manage not to fall back into warfare like just about every other country has done over there.

"How come Brazilians don't have racial problems?" he asked.

"We've got too many other problems," said Marisa. "Once we fix our economy and end poverty, and once we end government corruption, which *Papai* says is the root of all of our trouble, maybe then we'll start killing each other, but I don't think so. We'd be too busy dancing.

"Anyway, everybody here's all mixed up. We're all *viralatas*, mixed breeds. Almost everybody has at least an Indian grandpa or little black grandma somewhere in their line, unless they come from the South, which is mostly German and Italian. But anybody else? Forget it. We all have a foot in Africa. That's why we can samba!"

She laughed and launched into a seated dance.

Jack mused that what she said rang true. These people weren't at all patriotic, but they were fiercely proud to be Brazilian. They were cohesive in that way. *It must have more to do with a sense of family*, he thought, which to Brazilians was paramount and seemed to be color blind. Family was family, and Brazil, with all its faults, was the extended family that they shared.

He watched her move in the fire light that played along her slender form and highlighted the sensuousness of her features. He wanted her badly. He wished she were ten years older and that they had met under different circumstances. Watching her moving in the light and smiling from across the crackling flames sent an electricity buzzing through him in ecstatic misery. He felt like a eunuch sent to guard the sultan's harem, duty bound to look but not to touch. But then there was a difference—a eunuch couldn't feel what he was feeling. He envied them in that moment for not having the equipment that all men cherished, and which usually led them astray.

Jack, like most others, thought from below the belt at times, and the whole trip he'd been under constant attack from his lower train of thought. But he wasn't going to succumb to his baser instincts, not this time. This girl was too young, too vulnerable, and he liked her too much to add himself to her list of problems. But still he wanted her. He felt flush.

She stopped swaying and asked, "Where else do you like, Jack?"

He was happy for the question. Talking kept him occupied.

"I don't know, Marisa. I travel a lot for business reasons, so I never really seem to have a much time to look around. I've been out to Hawaii and down to the Bahamas and Mexico a few times on vacation. They're all beautiful—the beaches were nice, but something wasn't right for me. Everyone there's American. *Hell*, in Cancun it's hard to order a meal in Spanish. Everyone smiles at you and answers in perfect English.

"To tell you the truth, I think I like South Rio more than anywhere else. It's a real city. It has a pulse and a passion all its own, Leblon, Ipanema, Copacabana, Barra da Tijuca—they're beautiful and filled with handsome, charming people. It's a joy to go to Rio, even with all its crime and other problems, because it's real, not just some picturesque resort complex built by Disney and his seven thousand dwarves.

"I guess when I get on an airplane and fly out of Houston, I'd rather not see another American or anything American until I get back home. I don't want to eat at

McDonalds in Timbuktu; I want to eat fried monkey, if that's what they eat there."

"I don't like McDonald's either, Jack. The one in Cuiabá is too expensive, and the sandwiches are tiny. We hardly ever eat there. It just isn't worth it."

"That's right, Marisa. Remember, that. I'm glad to see that those cultural imperialists won't worm their way into your belly and your pocketbook."

"What?"

"Nothing. What's your favorite city?" he asked.

"I've never been anywhere but Poconé and Cuiabá, and I don't like either of them. My favorite city is Rio, just like you. I haven't been there in the flesh, but I go there all the time in my dreams. *Mamãe* has described everything there is to know about Leblon to me a million times since I was a little girl. That's where I'm going to live, just like my parents did before—in a nice apartment by the beach, and every morning I'll get up early and take a walk by the ocean to listen to the waves. *Mamãe* says that the sound of the ocean is very peaceful. She says it's the same sound that you hear when you put a big snail shell to your ear but bigger and never ending. Is that true, Jack?"

"Yes, it is, Marisa, but you'll know soon enough. Once we get your emeralds, I'll take you and your mother to Rio where you can decide for yourself."

"You forgot my father."

"Your father, too," he said, not believing it.

"It's going to be so wonderful to see Rio, Jack. Will you show me all the beaches?"

"Sure. It's a promise."

"Good!" She looked up at the rising moon. "Well, we should get some sleep. The sun will be up by five."

They stood and she raised up on tiptoes to kiss him goodnight on the cheeks. As she kissed him, he breathed in her scent and held her to him in passion for an instant. Then he caught himself, squeezed her arms fraternally and let her go. There was a hesitance, a question in her eyes, but it passed quickly, replaced by the usual traces of laughter.

"*Boa noite*, Jack."

"*Até amanha*, Marisa. Sleep well."

She had done just that, he remembered then as he plodded along the trail behind her. She slept peacefully and didn't even wake at the sound of a jaguar's growl far to the south. She slept while he twisted, restless in his hammock, and watched her until dawn.

It was the next day that she saved his life.

Clouds had scudded along in droves, and by dawn they filled the sky with threatening gray as the travelers broke camp and resumed their journey. Marisa knew immediately what they meant: the first of the scattered, heavy thunderstorms that harkened in the rainy season. There was no danger at the moment, other than in river bottoms where floodwaters like the ones that took her brothers could rumble through at any moment without warning. She knew that they were in for a deluge and that they were going to get wet, very wet.

The damn burst around 10 a.m. Lightening flashed and thundered through the sky in blue-white reproaches from an angered god. A tree, not more than twenty yards away, took a bolt dead center and split into kindling that caught fire despite the storm. Then the rain followed in blurring sheets that struck them heavy on the back like cataracts from heaven. They bent low in their saddles and shivered through the miles. It was late in the afternoon when Jack's horse spooked and threw him. It probably wouldn't have happened had it been a clear day, but it wasn't—it was miserable and wet, and he wasn't paying attention like he should have been, so he failed to see the large snake coiled in the path in time to stop his horse. Neighing loudly, his horse reared back, threw him and galloped quickly away, leaving Jack scrambling in the mud, face to face with a *surucucu*, a long and angry bushmaster, cocked back and ready to strike. He knelt there dazed and paralyzed, not wanting to move and startle the snake, and not wanting to stay within striking distance. He simply did not know what to do.

The snake was eyeing him evilly, flicking its tongue in calculation, when Marisa acted. She'd heard the horse behind her and turned in time to see Jack fall. In just a few seconds she galloped back toward him, pulling free a shovel from her saddle as she rode.

Jack didn't see her coming. All he saw were the slit eyes of the snake as it arched its neck back to strike and its flickering tongue that gauged the distance to its target. He didn't know if snakes could blink but he thought it did, and he remembered back to college Judo class, when he could always see a move coming in the eyes of his opponents. He tensed and readied to futilely jump back when the blade of a shovel caught the snake just behind its head. Down and down and down again came the merciless shovel until it decapitated the murderous, flailing reptile.

Marisa shoveled the head into the brush, then rushed to her friend. She knelt into the mud and hugged him, crying. "Are you all right, Jack. Did he bite you?" She was pale with fear.

"No. I'm all right, *querida*. My horse threw me, that's all. I thought for a moment that I had had it."

"He didn't bite you?"

"No. I'm fine. Honest."

She let out a sigh of relief.

"Good, I don't think I could have helped if he bit you, Jack. We don't have the antivenom. I'm glad you're okay."

He looked into her eyes and saw the fear and worry there turn to relief. He clutched her to him and breathed in deeply. "Thanks, Marisa. It looks like you saved my life. Thank you."

She clung to him, then stood and said with a smile, "And not only that. I caught our dinner!"

She walked back and proudly picked up the body of the bushmaster still twisting into itself like a pretzel.

Jack stood and couldn't help but laugh. "You mean you know how to cook one of those, too?"

"Of course. Who doesn't?"

After they gathered their horses, they journeyed on until they set up camp at sunset, several hours later. They dined that night on snake and rice *tropeiro*—snake with rice and cassava flour. Jack was glad to be alive and thought it was delicious. They spent the night together, dry under a tarp that Marisa set up better than a tent. Jack watched her breath as she slept with her head resting on his shoulder. He was thankful to be living, yet sad to be alive in the agony of passion.

That was just three days ago, he brooded as they rode to the end of their journey. The day was at hand. She said that they would reach the mine in the late afternoon. She was tense with anticipation and anxiety about finding her father.

Neither of them knew what lay ahead. It was a devil's dilemma for him. He knew that if her father was alive, he would never consent to his daughter dating him—he was thirty-eight after all and she just twenty-two. There was nothing to be done about it. He felt wrong for wanting her anyway, and besides even if they came together, how could it possibly work. Their lives were as different as a Bedouin's and an Eskimo's. No, he honestly hoped to find her father because he knew it would make her happy and that was what mattered most to him. He sighed.

He'd sighed a lot the last few weeks, a lifetime's worth of sighing. *Why did life have such wicked turns*, he wondered. He'd dated women of wealth and class in his country and elsewhere, even in Brazil, and he'd also walked his way through various far-flung whorehouses as a young man, but never had he felt anything like he was feeling now for this young girl, this Jane without a Tarzan who lugged him like a novice through the woods. He thought back to all those Johnny Weissmuller movies and felt oddly like the leading lady. He was sure that Marisa was more than a match for any caiman or anaconda and probably more than a match for him.

She had his heart in her hip pocket and didn't have a clue. Justice, he mulled, for the few hearts that he had broken. Wasn't there a law of physics that stated, "To each action there is an equal and opposite reaction?" Well, whichever one it was, payday was at hand.

She rode on ahead, as fresh as a springtime rose, and he watched her, loving her innocence and her mastery, a child and a woman, a killer and a saint. She was everything a man could want and more. She was too much.

He couldn't have her with the sanction of her family, he was sure. And even with it, he doubted he could keep her for long. She was more than a man could hope for, and certainly more than a man could hope to keep. She was one-of-a-kind. Unique. Like the famous emerald, the Heart of Brazil.

She was without equal, yet he felt she was somehow his responsibility no matter what would come. He would guarantee her future. He knew the world beyond the Pantanal, and he would repay his debt by helping her to know it. He would ensure her happiness, no matter what it cost him. He owed her that. He owed her his life, though as they were fast approaching the mine, he almost wished she hadn't killed the bushmaster.

She reined in her horse, and he drew up beside her. She pointed to the river that lie ahead.

"That's the border of Fonseca's land, Jack. We have to cross here."

"Well, let's go."

"We'll go, but I think we should check our animals first. It's late in the dry season, and it's not such a good idea to swim through the rivers. The piranhas are hungry. We'll be okay, but I'd like to look over the animals first. If they're bleeding because of saddle sores we could wind up in trouble fast."

She grabbed his hand and inspected it. It was fully scabbed but could still bleed easily.

"Keep this hand up out of the water, okay?"

"Sure, no problem." he responded.

"Good. Now, take off your saddle, and let's check your horse."

Jack unhitched and pulled off his saddle to examine his horse. He found nothing. After Marisa was done with her horses, she checked his, looking for saddle sores, festered bug bites or open scrapes around the fetlocks. She finished, satisfied.

"Well, I think we're all right. Let's cross. The mine's on the other side, just beyond that ridge."

It was the end of the trail. Answers lay just beyond, answers and an end to the way things were. Jack felt it was goodbye. There was the matter of her father, if he was even alive. The difference in their ages was too great, and he led a different life far away, entrenched in another continent.

All of this aside, if she felt even half the attraction he felt, she hadn't shown it. It was a unilateral romance all his own, *one of imagination*, he thought. His heart hurt, flooded with the passion that he couldn't let burst forth.

Whatever lay ahead, Jack would do what he could to help Marisa and her mother. She saved his life after all, and even if she had taken his heart casually, without even knowing it, and even if it was ripping him to pieces, Jack felt responsible. He would act in her best interest, and no matter what they found across the river, he'd see that she and her mother would be taken care of.

They saddled the horses and trotted down river to a low bank in a narrow bend.

"This is the best place to ford, Jack. Just ease your horse forward and let him do the work. *Pantaneira* horses are good swimmers. I'll go first, then you follow."

He pulled up to her and squeezed her arm and said, "Look Marisa, we don't know what we're going to find on the other side. I hope we find your dad."

"We will," she smiled bravely, but it was wooden. Uncertainty hung at the corners of her mouth and eyes, like subdued buntings.

He noted it with concern.

"Don't worry, Jack. I can handle whatever comes, but I always hope for the best. We'll find him. You'll see."

This time her smile was real.

"Where do you get your optimism," he asked, more to himself than to her.

"From my father. Things will be fine, Jack. You'll see. But thanks for caring."

She leaned over and kissed him, not on the cheek but on the lips. His eyes closed with her touch. When they opened, he thought for a moment that he caught a trace of something other than friendship in her expression, but she turned away too quickly for him to be sure.

"Let's go," she said.

She kicked her horse into the river and tugged the pack horse in behind her. They walked about ten feet in before they lost bottom and began to swim. She was right: the horses swam strongly, without concern. Jack followed her in, and they were soon across. The horses struggled up the other, steeper bank, then shook the water from their manes.

Marisa dismounted and said, "Let's walk them up above the ridge. We're not far from the mine, and we can unsaddle them and let them dry out once we get there."

"Whatever you think, Trail Boss."

She smiled and moved on. They climbed the easy slope slowly, neither of them knowing what lay beyond or what to expect. They were both surprised by what they found there.

Chapter Six

A large chain-link fence, at least seven feet tall and topped with concertina wire met them as they topped the ridge. It shined with newness and rolled out east and west until it fell from view.

"This didn't used to be here," exclaimed Marisa. "The last time I was here there wasn't even barbed wire—the river keeps the cattle in. Why would anybody spend the money to build a fence like this?"

"To keep people out," answered Jack.

"This is very strange. Nobody ever comes out this way, except to round up cattle for market in March. There's nothing here to protect. There's nothing worth stealing."

Jack thought the emeralds were worth stealing, but he didn't say so. He looked through the fence for signs of cattle or range riders. There was nothing in sight but scrub thicket, trees, and of course, huge clusters of birds around scattered ponds farther in the distance. He didn't relish the thought of cutting through the fence, out in the wilderness where justice was private, summary and often dealt-out with a gun, but there was no other way.

He swallowed. "I guess we'll have to cut through."

Marisa, who had walked a little way down the ridge, looked over to him from where she was standing.

"It looks like someone already has."

She pointed to a wired-in patch big enough for a horse to pass through.

Jack walked over and examined the patch. It was fresh, with no signs of rust. It couldn't have been a month old, but he couldn't really tell because the fence was also new and rust-free.

New as it was, though, someone had recently been through it. Probably Heiner, he thought. He searched through their equipment and pulled out a pair of pliers with wire cutters in the head—something listed in the stores that Marisa had asked him to buy in Cuiabá. He hadn't seen the necessity when he bought them, but now he was glad she'd insisted.

"Were you planning to cut through some fences?" he asked as he knelt down to start snipping.

She shrugged.

"You never know. Better to be safe than sorry."

Jack cut the wire that formed the patch and carefully unlooped it.

"We'll patch the fence back like it was before we leave here. I don't want anybody knowing we came through."

"Me neither. It doesn't look like *Senador* Fonseca likes visitors."

After half-an-hour spent unlooping the wire, Jack pulled the patch back to clear the opening, and Marisa walked the horses through.

"The mine's just over there."

Marisa pointed north to a small hummock about a mile away. They mounted the horses and trotted toward it, Marisa coaxing the packhorse to match the pace.

Upon reaching the base of the small hill, they slipped off, unsaddled their horses and let them roam free to graze and dry out. Then they moved their equipment under the shade of the trees that clothed the rise, to keep it out of view of any passing range rider.

Marisa got her bearings and led Jack to the entrance. She was surprised to find it blocked with the tailings she had helped her father dig out six months before.

"It's here, Jack," she said, pointing to the mound of gray earth and rocks that filled the outline of a hole set in the ground. He kneeled down to grab a handful of soil, which he examined. It was gray and clayish, a talc schist similar to that of the Santa Terezinha deposit seven hundred miles away to the north of Brasília. He felt the clayish loam in his hand. It could definitely be emerald-bearing soil, much different than the rest of the earth they passed over on their journey. His pulse quickened.

Marisa looked down at the mine entrance nervously.

"I guess *Papai* must have filled it in to keep away the curious."

"Describe the shaft to me, Marisa. What are we looking at here? A vertical drop?"

It might take a man months to re-dig a vertical shaft. The prospect didn't please him.

"No. It starts out vertical, but after about five feet, it turns to a horizontal decline and tunnels toward the center of the hill until it breaks into the main shaft. This is an access shaft that *Papai* dug to break into the original. The earth is loose, so I doubt it would take us very long to dig it out. A few hours maybe, that's all."

Jack looked at his watch. It was just past noon.

"Well, I guess we'd better get started."

They walked back to their equipment and grabbed their shovels and a pickax. Then they started digging. Marisa was silent while she worked. She seemed worried that the mine was sealed and that her father wasn't waiting there to greet them. It wasn't part of her plan. It hadn't occurred to her that he wouldn't be there, or she hadn't let it occur to her. Doubts were starting to form, and she became more anxious with every shovel of clay that flew back over her shoulder.

Jack noticed her anxiety, but couldn't really think of much to say to reassure her. He didn't like the fence they had cut through at all. If someone had gone to the trouble to erect it, they would surely patrol it. Proof of that lay in the fact that it had been recently patched.

He wanted to be in and out of there fast. His nerves were on edge, and he was digging as fast as he could. Clay dust billowed up like a cloud around them, sticking on their clothes still soaked with river water and mixing duskily with their sweat. It was hot, miserable work, but the dirt was loose and shoveled easily. They were down four feet in less than three hours.

Marisa had gone back to their bags to fetch a water bottle while Jack dug on. He was moving faster because, according to Marisa, he should soon hit the horizontal decline. He sunk his shovel in the loose gray earth and it met resistance. Trying again, he drove his foot down hard upon the shovel's shank, but it didn't cut through what blocked it. *Most likely a root*, he thought. He bent down and started clearing away the clay with his fingers.

The overpowering smell of death choked him the moment he clasped the decaying hand. He fell back and scrambled away from the claw that strained for the surface. Jack jumped out of the hole and lay there panting, gagging on the smell and on the bile that forced its way up from his stomach in galling, nauseous retches.

"What's the matter, Jack?" asked Marisa as she approached him with the water.

"Nothing, nothing. Just the heat, I guess."

"Yeah, it's hot isn't it?

She wiped her sweaty, dirty brow. She had dried from the river crossing but was now bathed in sweat, and her breasts showed through her moist and muddy shirt. He didn't notice. He was terrified with the death below them that he had touched, and which clung to his fingers. And he was even more terrified of her reaction to the decayed hand that probably belonged to her father.

"You look overheated, Jack. Why don't you take a break and let me dig awhile? We're almost there. I can dig out the rest."

"No!" He almost shouted, and instantly jumped to his feet. "I mean, no. There are more important things for you to do. I'm worried about the horses. Why don't you go check to see if they're all right? I'll finish up here. I'm fine. Just a little hot, that's all."

"Are you sure? You're acting kind of funny."

"That's because I'm worried about the horses."

"Why worry about the horses? We've left them alone to graze by themselves the entire trip. Why worry now?"

"I don't know. I've just got a bad feeling, all right?" He raised his voice without meaning to. "Could you go get them and bring them in under the trees? Could you please just do that for me?"

"Sure, Jack, sure." She seemed hurt and irritated, but left to do as he asked.

He looked back into the pit to see the bloody hand staring up at him, as if trying to claw its way back to life. He felt sick, but he had work to do. He splashed some water on the bandanna he kept in his back pocket, tied it tight around his nose and mouth and then jumped back in the hole. He dug around the hand and slowly excavated another—it, too, clawing toward the light—followed by two arms and shoulders.

Finally, with a sweep of his shaking fingers, Jack unearthed a face.

It was a face turned upward with a look of pure feral terror, like that of a bilge rat trapped in the boiler room of a sinking ship, a terror he had seen before and hoped to never see again. It was a man who had been buried alive, screaming wildly into the dirt that bound and suffocated him, and which even filled his open mouth. It was a man he knew. It was Heiner.

Jack's revulsion turned to pity and even a sense of loss. The decay of this man who had once been his rival filled his lungs, but he didn't choke on it.

Instead, he choked on the loss he felt for the man he'd met in every forlorn corner of the world, who almost always managed to outsmart him, outbid him and get there first. This last time Heiner had beaten him again.

Jack was sad, because when all the chips were counted, they were always friends. He thought of the large and friendly woman, Frau Klimt, Heiner's mother whom he had met in Idar Oberstein, Heiner's hometown in Germany. He had spent a week with them several years earlier while searching for a cutter for a very special order—a candelabra of pure rock crystal.

Heiner had taken him in and had been the perfect host. A friendship formed that was never broken in all the following years of the German's hard bargaining, conniving and sometimes underhanded business practices. Heiner was Heiner to all who really knew him, and they accepted him, faults and all, for what he was—an unscrupulous but big and boisterous teddy bear.

Jack took a moment, standing over the horror that was once his friend, praying for him and asking his forgiveness for what he had to do. Then he breathed in deep, held his breath and struggled the body up and out of its grave. His remorse was tempered by the sound he heard in his mind, that big rumbling chuckle of Heiner's that assured him his friend would have done the same, had circumstances been different.

Jack dragged Heiner away from the mine entrance and laid him down gently beneath a tree where he covered his face with their burlap tool sack. He said another quick prayer, then pulled loose the leather satchel slung across the body's shoulder. Jack opened it, peered inside and was stunned at what he saw.

The satchel was full of emerald rough that weighed at least five pounds—over one hundred thousand carats!

Jack's legs felt weak as he shuffled back to the edge of the hole, where he sat with his legs dangling down. He reached inside the satchel and sifted the rocks through his fingers. They were all exquisite, well-formed crystals with a slightly bluish green color that soothed the eyes like nothing else could. The majority of them were large, large enough to yield five carats, and the largest were much larger. Jack reached his fingers through the stones until they stopped short, halted with the tactile knowledge of having felt a stone beyond all others.

Jack's heart pounded as he withdrew the large crystal and then nearly stopped when he beheld it. This emerald was perfect in shape and form and color, as perfect as the others only larger, much larger. It weighed heavy in his palm like a can of peas.

Hoping beyond expectation, he held it to the light—he could see right through it! It had the transparency and color of a coral lagoon, with hardly a blemish. His hand shook as he hefted it to gauge its weight, easily six hundred carats. If the stone was truly as clean as it looked, its raw form might yield a cut stone of two hundred to three hundred carats, more than twice the size of the Heart of Brazil, the most famous emerald in the world, and it looked to be as clean! He wouldn't know until it came back from the cutter, but it looked very good. He was buzzing with excitement and trying to estimate the emerald's value when he heard Marisa scream.

Jack jumped to his feet and ran to where she stood near the body of his friend. He reached out to comfort her, but she pushed away, repelled—he was ripe with the scent of death.

"Marisa! Marisa, it's okay. It's all right."

He tried to draw her to him, but she pushed away again. On seeing the leather pouch, she grabbed it from him and clutched to her chest, crying even harder.

"It's okay, Marisa. Listen to me!"

He gripped her arms and shook her. "It's okay! It's not your dad. Listen to me!"

He shook her again.

"It's all right. It's not your father!"

"It's his bag! It's his specimen bag! We gave it to him for his birthday."

"But that's not his body. That's Heiner. Believe me."

She trembled with shock and grief, clutching the pouch as sobs racked through her. Then, stench or not, she clung to him. "It's not *Papai*? Are you sure?"

"I'm sure, Marisa. It's not your father. It's my friend, Heiner."

"But what about the bag? It's my father's. He must have been here. Where is he?"

"I don't know, Marisa, but I'll try to find out."

"When I saw the body and the bag, I thought it was *Papai*," she sobbed. "Where can he be, Jack? Where is my father?"

"I don't know, *querida*, but we'll find him. We'll find him."

He hugged her to him and stroked her hair with his muddied hands, hoping desperately that they wouldn't find her father in the mine. Jack slowly comforted her and when she was calm enough, he walked down to their supplies to retrieve flashlights and a kerosene lantern.

He returned to see her staring down into the shaft.

"I guess I'd better go inside and have a look around, Marisa. Why don't you stay here and rest."

"No, I need to go with you, Jack. There's a deep vertical shaft just inside, not far from the entrance, and you could fall in if you're not careful. And I need to know if my father's in there. I need to know. Come on. I know the way."

She took a flashlight and jumped down into the hole. When Jack removed the body, he had cleared an opening they could pass through. Marisa started to wriggle inside, but Jack stopped her.

"Just a minute. Let's put the lantern through first to see if there is oxygen."

He lit it and pushed it into the hole where it flamed brightly without sputtering.

"It looks good," he said.

She nodded, then inched herself into the tunnel. He followed behind her. They gagged on the fetid air inside, still heavy with Heiner's decay. It was cramped and had not been dug for walking. It angled down steeply for about thirty feet and then opened into a larger, horizontal shaft that led away in two directions, wide but not very high—the ceiling barely cleared Jack's head. Marisa held up her hand in a signal to stop while she shone her light down on the floor around them. Not more than five feet to the left was a deadfall centered in the shaft and at least three-quarters of its width. She picked up a pebble and tossed it in. There was silence for a few seconds, until it clattered to rest far below.

"You wouldn't want to fall in there," she said gravely. "I don't know how deep it is, but you can't see the bottom."

She waved her light into the hole, but it revealed nothing but darkness.

"We go around it. There's nothing over there." She pointed to the right. "It's pretty much played out, but this side's still rich. Be careful, Jack. I doubt I could get you out if you fell in."

She edged around the pit carefully, skirting it with her back to the wall. He followed her slowly, heels to the wall and toes over the abyss. She was right, he thought nervously: he could have easily stepped into the hole that gaped beneath them while he was checking the wall for crystals. He would have to pay more attention.

Once they were around it, Marisa picked up her pace, though still cautious. As they moved deeper down the tunnel, Jack began to see hints of green crystals, gleaming in the gray talc of the shaft. He stopped at one of the larger ones and managed to pry it loose with his fingers. The hexagon glowed in the lamp light. Like the contents of the bag, it was exquisite.

Jack shivered with the excitement of knowing that the stones he carried on his shoulder made them millionaires. Dread at what had happened to Heiner, however, quickly overshadowed him. His mind flipped through thoughts like the pages of a pulp horror novel.

Someone had buried his friend alive, but who and why? And why didn't they take the stones he was carrying? It didn't make sense. Where was The Professor? Would they find him further down the shaft?

He walked on, grim. The curse of the Borba mine lived, and they were walking in its bowels. Would they escape it? They were treading on dangerous ground, and they needed to leave as quickly as possible.

The green glints in the tunnel walls lost their charm. Would this be their tomb, too? He was pondering this when he bumped into Marisa, who had stopped and was shining her light onto a bundle up ahead. She was shaking. It looked to be a body.

Jack hugged her and said, "Stay here."

The stench of it hit him like a wall as he moved toward it. It was the body of a strong, wiry man with his hands tied behind his back, a bullet through his head and several more through his torso. It looked like a botched execution.

Jack took a deep breath and knelt down to roll the body over and get a look at its face. The forehead was gone, but the face was still mostly intact. He breathed a sigh of relief. It wasn't The Professor, unless he had changed greatly since he took the picture that Itzhak had on file. Even twenty years in the Pantanal couldn't change race, and this man was dark black. Who was he, Jack wondered?

"It's not your father, Marisa! It's somebody else. Who, I don't know."

Marisa walked up tentatively, still afraid to look. But once she did, she had answers. "That's Fabrício Rocha. He's an old-time *zagaieiro* from Poconé. I wonder what he's doing here?"

"What's a *zagaieiro*?" asked Jack as he backed away from the corpse.

"A jaguar hunter. Fabrício is one of the last few living, or at least he was."

"Why, because jaguar hunting is illegal?"

"No, they don't care about that. No, there aren't many *zagaieiros* anymore because they used to hunt jaguars with spears. One man, his dogs, one spear, one big cat. It's a high-risk occupation, and kids these days aren't much interested in it. There are better things to do. I wonder who did this to him. I can't imagine him letting anybody tie him up and shoot him."

"Well, it looks like he put up a fight. Somebody emptied a gun in him before they put him down. Let's get out of here, Marisa. I don't want to end up like that."

He pointed down to the corpse of the old hunter.

"Not yet, Jack. We still have a lot of tunnel to check. I want to find my father if he's here."

Her eyes began to water.

"Okay, sure. But once we've checked the tunnel, we get on our horses and get out of here. It's dangerous to be here now. Somebody doesn't want this mine discovered."

She nodded and walked on deeper into the mine in defiance of its curse. They covered the entire mine in little over an hour. They found some of The Professor's gear, but not a trace of him.

It was almost evening when they returned to the surface. It had been a rough time below. Marisa half-expected to find the body of her father with every turn the mineshaft took, and now upon returning to the surface, she felt worse for not knowing, for not having an end to this mystery, for having nothing against which she could summon a deep resolve.

One way or another, she had hoped to find her father, but she hadn't. And she had no idea where else to look. She felt awful and weak. Why had her father finally been granted his wish to find the Borba mine after twenty years of searching, only to be drawn-in by its curse and vanish like all the *bandeirantes* before him? It seemed so unfair.

The lives of her brothers had been lost in the gold mining that bankrolled their sustained search. Her mother had given up everything she loved to follow her husband while he pursued his quest, only to lose him on the eve of their success, after having sacrificed her life and the lives of their children for the cause. *Where was he?* she wondered. *Where could he be?*

It was too much. The fear. The bodies. The disappointment and relief. It was just too much. She sat beside the mine entrance, hugging her knees to her chest, crying like a baby. It all came out then. Her sadness for the loss of her father, for her brothers, the months of being steadfast and propping up her mother when she felt like dying inside and losing her mind, too. It all rushed forth in a torrent of tears.

Jack sat down beside her and gathered her to him. He stroked her hair and offered sympathy reserved for those one loves. His heart poured out in silence, bathing her in his compassion and strength. She cried for at least half an hour, then recovered as quickly as she had broken down. The spirit born in her of her father returned, the eternal optimist. She sniffed away her tears and smiled an apology for weakness.

"He wasn't in the mine, Jack, so he must be alive. That's good. I just wish I knew where to find him."

"I'll do everything I can to help you find him, *querida*, but first you and I need to get out of here. Listen, if you're feeling all right, I'd like you to get our gear packed and the horses saddled up while I bury my friend and get this mine sealed back up again like it was. I don't want whoever it was that did this to Heiner to know that we've been here, and I want to be across the river and far away before we bed down tonight."

He brushed her cheek and smiled.

"All right?"

"Okay, Jack, I'll do just what you ask."

"Good."

She smiled a brave smile, braver than she felt, and got up to leave.

As she turned from him, he said, "Marisa."

"Yes, Jack?" She looked back.

"With the emeralds you have in that sack, you're a millionaire—in American money. You and your mom can now go to Rio and live in style!"

She smiled, but it was empty of anything and both of them knew it.

As soon as she was gone from view, Jack went over to his friend. He was out of practice, but he searched his mind and came up with a few prayers of eulogy that he whispered quickly. Then he held his breath and heaved up the corpse.

Heiner was a big man, and as dead weight, he was almost too much to move after such an exhausting day. Jack rushed to ease his friend back into his grave before he had to breathe again and suck in the putrescence. As he moved the body back to its grave, he thought he felt the eyes of Heiner on him, not the dead eyes of the corpse but the living eyes of his old friend.

Wherever he was, Jack knew that Heiner was laughing, laughing for having beat him to the mine, and laughing gleefully now, happy as an imp for putting him through this misery. Jack slid him in the hole and started to chuckle. As always, when he was mad enough to explode and felt like smashing the German's nose for having outsmarted or plain outright cheated him, the German would laugh his disarming laugh and somehow make them friends again. It was just a game to Heiner, and they both knew it. Jack would miss him.

He said a final prayer and began to fill in the hole. Tears fell freely from Jack's eyes as he shoveled dirt into the hole and said his last goodbyes. He smiled through the tears and laughed again, for he knew wherever he went when this life was over, Heiner would be there waiting with a smile and a beer. Heiner always bought the beer, with a backslap and a laugh. It was the least he could do, he always said.

Just as Jack was tamping down the grave, Marisa came back to tell him that the horses were ready to be saddled. They looked to each other and hugged without a word. It had been a draining day for both.

When they reached the bottom of the hill and saddled up, the sun was just a crescent on the earth, a lemon peel dropped from heaven. They galloped through the orange light toward the menace of the perimeter fence. If it hadn't been sunset, and if they hadn't been momentarily blinded by the flame of dying light and numbed by what they had just been through, they probably would have seen the truck rushing toward them in time to have headed back into the copse around the hill to escape detection, but they didn't see it.

In fact, they were so self-absorbed that the first sign of trouble they noticed was a burst of automatic rifle fire, which brought them back to earth. Then it was a race.

Jack screamed to Marisa, "The fence! MAKE THE FENCE!

Then he spurred his tired mount and rode low in the saddle. He drove the horse to its limits, and the fence drew nearer by the hoof-fall. Rifle fire pocked continually behind them like popcorn in a popper, but he willed himself to ignore it. He knew that the fence and the river would buy them enough time for a head start, and he knew that the men who had buried his friend alive would show no mercy. He worried about Marisa, though, and that was what caused him to look back.

He could see her maybe fifty yards behind him, galloping her horse for all it was worth. She was concentrated and brave, but it wasn't enough—her horse took a spray of bullets in its forequarters and tumbled out from beneath her, throwing her headlong into a thorn bush.

The truck was raging toward her in a bumping, screeing fury of rubber on dry earth, but that didn't deter Jack. He swung around and spurred his horse toward her. She lay still while he and the truck approached, and he feared her dead.

But just as he drew near, she stirred and sat upright. He screamed to her to get up and be ready to mount, but she was stunned and didn't understand. She sat there dazed, which forced him to rein-in and dismount. As soon as he did, machine gun fire cut the legs out from under his horse. It fell in a flurry of whinnies, but the bullets soon silenced it. Jack stood before Marisa as a human shield and raised his hands in surrender.

The truck pulled up in seconds, and four men armed with machine guns jumped out from the bed.

He managed to say, "Excuse me; we are lost," just before he was clubbed to earth with a rifle butt. Then all was darkness.

Chapter Seven

T he blackness rumbled and bumped the senses. Dim red light loomed far away beyond the tremors like an awakening volcano yawning up to fill the void with burning, angry magma. With a jolt of pain jabbed hard in his forehead, Jack came to, moaning in Marisa's lap.

"Aggh...Where am I?" he asked, trying to focus on her face as she bounced above him.

"In the truck," she whispered back. "Are you okay? You've been out for over an hour."

He moaned again as the truck bottomed-out on a low spot. "I'm okay. How about you?"

"I'm scared, Jack. What are they going to do with us?"

"I don't know."

He sat up, massaging his throbbing head, then put an arm around Marisa while he focused and studied their captors. They weren't the cowhands or *peões* one normally encountered on a Brazilian ranch.

These men were too well dressed and too well coiffed. Decked out in silver-toed boots and gold chains, they looked more like Cuban real estate agents during the boom years in Miami. They were as out of place in the Pantanal as he was, and so were their weapons. One guy held a loose bead on them with an M-16, while another held an F.A.L .308 assault rifle resting in his lap. These weren't the guns of backland hunters. These were the guns of war. And they were illegal for civilians to own in Brazil.

There were two other men in the cab, both similarly armed. Things didn't look good. As his fog began to lift, Jack tried to figure out who they were, where they might be taking them and why they had killed Heiner and his guide. Something didn't fit.

He could understand their killing of Heiner, but why didn't they keep the bag of emeralds? The emeralds would be worth millions once they were cut. It didn't make any sense.

He looked to Marisa, who was staring nervously into her lap. He regretted then that he had involved her in this. He wanted to save her, somehow, but on looking at their captors, he knew his chances were slim. "Where are you taking us?" he asked.

"Shut your mouth," said the evil-looking man with the M-16. "You'll find out when we get there."

And they did, forty minutes later when the truck passed several outbuildings to pull up and park behind a large white-stuccoed ranch house.

"Get out," commanded their guard.

They were led inside by the man who sat in the cab beside the driver, with the others following them and holding their guns at the ready. They walked through a sprawling living room, past a large table covered with newspapers and graphs, to a desk where a man was seated working at a computer.

"Father," said the leader, "we caught more trespassing *garimpeiros*."

The man turned from the screen to look around. *Senador* Afonso Fonseca de Cabral, the favored presidential candidate, glared at them as he stood.

He took the bag his son offered and dumped it out on his desk. Hundreds of crystals poured forth into a glinting pile. Fonseca picked up the biggest of the crystals, the one Jack thought bigger than the Heart of Brazil, and held it in his hand. Anger smoldered in the darkness of his eyes, which were different than they were on campaign posters. They weren't fatherly. They were sinister and snake-like; coiled behind the ridge of his nose, they looked as if they wanted to strike out on their own. The warm paper smile that was plastered on every wall throughout the country was missing, replaced instead by a thin-lipped scowl cut sharp below the line of his narrow mustache.

"Who told you about the mine?" he demanded.

"We came looking for Professor Fontes," replied Jack honestly.

"Well, it looks as if you found him and his bag full of my stolen emeralds."

"We didn't find The Professor."

"Oh no? That's surprising. I had him sealed up in my mine after he signed a withdrawal form for the money he earned on the other emeralds he stole from me."

Marisa colored and shouted, "You killed my father?"

She tried to run forward and lash out, but one of the senator's henchmen grabbed her and pinned her arms to her sides.

Fonseca stepped close to her. "So you're his daughter, eh? You'd be pretty wouldn't you, if we cleaned you up a little and got rid of that smell. I'll consider having that done."

Marisa spit on him. He wiped his face then smiled. "I like spirit," he said, then slapped her hard across the face and added, "Do you?"

Jack lunged at him, but was brought up short with a rifle barrel jabbed into his neck. The dark man with his finger on the trigger shook his head in a clear warning against making any other movements.

Marisa was shaking with rage.

"What did you do with my father?" she shouted.

"I sealed him in my mine. It seemed fitting. I'm surprised you didn't find him. We stuck three in there last count. Two we buried alive, but one wouldn't give us the chance. That old *zagaieiro* nearly bit off José's head, didn't he José?"

The tall, dark henchman answered, "*Sim, Patrão*," as he rubbed his shoulder that ached with the memory.

Fonseca turned to his son.

"You'd better check on Professor Fontes, Hernanie. Maybe that gopher managed to dig his way out. He did like to dig."

"Yes, Father," said the son who, although slightly taller and without a receding hairline or expanding gut, was a mirror image of his father.

"Who else knows about my mine?" Fonseca asked Marisa.

She shook with anger and hatred, and wouldn't answer. He slapped her again, this time harder.

"A lot of people know," answered Jack, hoping to draw Fonseca's attention to himself. "A lot of people including the police in Rio and Cuiabá!"

"Well, the police aren't a problem. Let the others come if they want to. There's plenty of room for more in the mine." He looked closely at Jack. "You're not Brazilian, are you?"

"No, I'm not. I'm an American, and I represent a very large jewelry firm who will come looking for me if I disappear. If you're not careful, you'll have the American embassy breathing down your neck. Is that what you want?"

"Why not? They are already breathing down my neck. I have to listen to those condescending, meddling idiots all day long in Brasília, now that I'm going to be president. I've promised those fools all sorts of things—political and economic reform, land reform, protection of the Amazon. I promise them whatever they want, and they love me for it. If they're too gullible to realize that I couldn't possibly do half of what I've promised them even if I wanted to, that's their problem not mine. But for now, I'm their man. The ambassador and I are quite friendly. Too bad you won't have a chance to meet him. He's a blathering fool like most Americans, but he does throw a nice party, and he's promised lots of new loans to help support my 'Reform Package'."

Fonseca burst into laughter.

"Why are you doing this, Senator?" questioned Jack sincerely. "Why don't you let the people mine your land? It's no good for farming. It barely supports cattle. Why don't you let some of the people around here benefit from these emeralds? You're protected by law and entitled to fifty percent of all profits. There is easily a million dollars in rough right here, sitting on your desk. Why don't you want it sold? It just doesn't make any sense."

"Ah, once again a big mouth American is telling me what makes sense in Brazil. All I hear from your diplomats is how we do things backward and how badly we run our country. And every year they lean harder and harder on us, trying to bend us to their model. Their model, where everyone has everythin,g but no one really has anything. And those few who do manage to build a fortune have to struggle constantly to keep it safe for their children. Competition and commerce are the buzzwords of America. Well, we don't need competition here. My family has owned this land for almost three hundred years, and we own many other *fazendas* just like it. My ancestors were officers in the original *bandeiras* that settled Mato Grosso, and I own half the land between here and Cuiabá. Do you really think that I want to see my ancestral lands invaded by a bunch of illiterate, ill-smelling *garimpeiros*? I don't need them to mine my land, anyway. I could have a hundred of my peons digging there tomorrow if I wanted to, all happy to do anything I ask of them for nothing but food and a roof to live under.

You know what I pay them?"

"I don't," mumbled Jack.

"Nothing! I don't pay them anything at all in currency. But I give them everything they need to be happy—food, shacks, cane liquor and the occasional *forró* dance. And yet they love me. They love me the way the English used to love the King. I am king here, and I will soon be King of Brazil—president in name only. I plan to fix this country. Since the military stepped down, things have definitely headed south for the landed class in this country, but I plan to change that. We will regain our hold upon the land and put the rabble back in its place, rabble like that geology professor who snuck in here and nearly upset my operation, and who imported rabble like you."

Fonseca's fingers curled around the crystal he was holding, then he swung his fist up and caught Jack squarely in the jaw. Jack fell to his knees in a near swoon, still feeling the effects of his earlier concussion. As Jack knelt, cradling his throbbing head, the senator's foot connected under his chin, sending him backward to the ground like a failed punt.

"That felt good," he said to his son, who was grinning. "Take this pile of American shit back to the mine and bury him in it. But first look around for the body of Professor

Fontes. I want to know he's dead. And, listen, put those emeralds around the neck of our friend here. He likes emeralds, and I've always been one to give the people what they want."

Fonseca smiled and looked down to his hand. The crystal he held, larger than the rest, caught the light and glinted brightly with the color of money. His eyes narrowed with calculating greed.

"I'll keep this one," he said. "It would befit the new first lady to have an emerald larger than the Queen of Portugal has."

"Yes, it would," agreed his eldest son. Fonseca gripped his boy on the shoulder. "Get this trash out of here, Hernanie, and leave two men out there by the mine. I guess we'd better guard it from now on. Then get back here when you can. I need you to copy the tapes with our expanded distribution schedule. I still can't work that damn computer very well and have no time to learn. Our friends in Columbia will want a copy when they deliver the next shipment. They need advanced notice in order to scale up production."

"Yes, father," Hernanie said. He motioned to two of the men, and they hustled Jack out the door. He stopped just as he was about to leave and asked. "What about the girl? Do you want to bury her alive, too?"

"No, my son. I think I'll have a little fun with her first. She'll be here for you when you get done with your computer work, if I don't kill her. It's a good thing your mother took your brother and sister to Orlando, isn't it?"

"I'll say."

Hernanie grinned, then left.

Fonseca watched his son's exit with mixed emotions. It was good to be a father, but with Hernanie it had never been an easy task. The boy had never been right. He wanted his son to assume the management of their ranch operations when he assumed the presidency, but the boy would have to be watched to keep him from snorting all their merchandise. He had always dreamed that Hernanie would follow his footsteps and be president one day, but it didn't seem likely. Maybe his younger son would do better. Fonseca wondered where he had gone wrong.

He turned to his remaining man and said, "Clean up this little swamp flower, then put her in my bed. You can get some of my daughter's things for her to wear."

"*Sim, Patrão.*" The thug shouldered his weapon and dragged Marisa, kicking and screaming, away.

Chapter Eight

F or the second time in a night, pain welcomed Jack to consciousness in the back of a bouncing truck. This time though, he didn't awake to a concerned look from Marisa. He awoke to the leers of his executioners. He was skittering and sliding up against the tailgate while Hernanie and José were sitting on the wheel wells inside the truck bed, talking to each other and smoking cigarettes.

As Jack gained his senses, he took inventory of himself and of his situation. His face was swollen, and it felt like a watermelon in a microwave. His eyes were clearing and coming into focus, and with their focus came his reason— he had to find a way to save himself and then to rescue Marisa. He looked at the two men and their automatic rifles and knew it wouldn't be easy.

But he had to take a chance.

He'd rather take a bullet in the gut and bleed to death than die digging his way out of a grave like Heiner had. But what could he do? He watched them squatting on the wheel wells, both with their fingers in the trigger guards, and knew he didn't have a chance. Maybe if he jumped out of the truck and ran for the brush. No that wouldn't work. They'd have him trapped in the headlights in a minute and shoot him down like a jackrabbit. No, he'd have a better chance once they were all out of the truck, but not *much* of a chance.

He stared at the truck bed and watched the dust and pebbles jump and bounce atop the steel as the pickup raced toward his end. This wasn't what he had hoped for, but then who gets to pick? Well, whatever happened, he'd fight them at the entrance and force them to shoot him before he'd let them bury him alive. The absolute horror in Heiner's face ran up and down his spine like fingers. He shivered.

The truck struck something, probably one of the thousands of termite mounds that dotted the plain like stalagmites, and when it hit, he flew upward and then landed on something hard that knocked out his breath for a moment. He sat up and pulled at the offending something—it was The Professor's emerald pouch. Fonseca apparently wanted them back where he had found them. *A pity*, he thought.

Jack loved emeralds, and he thought of all of the beautiful jewels he could make with the crystals in the pouch. He thought of the necklace he had designed for his customer in Houston, and he thought of it lying on Marisa's chest, dangling down into her cleavage in a spray of diamond accents. He thought of her clothed only in the necklace, lying on a bed of satin, bathed in moonlight and the whispers of the ocean. He swallowed, and his pain was overwhelmed with the knowledge that he would never have the chance of seeing her like that, nor would any other deserving man.

These bastards were going to kill her and end any chance she had of living the dreams she cherished. It was unfair. It wasn't right. But what could he do?

The men riding in the bed of the truck with him were still preoccupied with resettling themselves after the jolt.

Jack flipped open the leather satchel and looked inside. In the moonlight, he could see the crystals and could even detect a slight trace of color. He had an idea. Maybe he could hook them with greed. Why not? Las Vegas, with its glitter and lure of easy money, brought people in by the millions. Why not these emeralds, too?

Capricious Lady Luck had no wheel to spin in this endeavor, but the glitz in these stones was real. They weren't the rhinestones of a high-stepping cabaret dancer, they were distilled wealth , greener than dollars and better able to weather time. He formed a plan and prayed for a chance of success.

Jack sat as still as he could in the rumbling pickup and studied the men before him. In the moonlight, Hernanie looked as evil as his father, as petulant and cruel but much less substantial.

Something about him was jackal-like. His posture? He was hunched over and thin. Or maybe his leering, shining eyes were like those of a coyote at the fence? Like a jackal he looked ready to snap at the heels of the weak or dying. Like a jackal he looked ready to dodge away from or toady-up to the lion, or anyone bigger than himself. He was in charge here only in name, only because he was the son of the strong man. It seemed to Jack as he watched them, that the other man was more in command. Hernanie reminded him of a fresh lieutenant discussing troop movements with a patient master sergeant.

Jack couldn't tell anything about the driver, but it seemed to him that the man across from Hernanie, was the man he needed to deal with. He was tall like Hernanie, but less gangly. He was fuller and straighter. And though he, too, seemed to be an ugly character—it was he, after all, who clubbed Jack on the head when they caught him—he didn't seem vicious for viciousness sake. He seemed to turn it on and off as necessary, like a power tool. Jack also imagined that once he turned it on, he wouldn't turn it off again until it had served its purpose. Jack knew that if he tried something and failed, that he would have to pay the final price.

"Hey," he called out above the rumble and crash of the truck.

"What do you want, *morto*?" asked Hernanie with a sneer.

"I want to make a deal."

"A deal? I don't think you're in much of a position to make a deal. What do you want? Wanna give me a blow job for your freedom?" Hernanie cackled at his joke. The other man smiled slightly to acknowledge it.

"No, I want to give you emeralds for a chance to disappear." Jack took a chance and tossed the pouch to the man who sat across from Hernanie. Fonseca's son brought his gun up at Jack's movement.

"Make another move like that, and I'll kill you."

Jack raised his hands.

"Good. That's the way, you faggot *gringo*. That's the way. I'd rather put you down your rat hole where you can dig a little first, than take a chance of getting your shitty guts all over our

nice truck. Right, José?"

He grinned over to the man across from him who was staring into the pouch.

"Right, Hernanie...right..." José said, then looked up. "You know, it's a shame to keep burying these emeralds back in the ground all the time. Maybe we should keep them."

"Father said to bury them."

"I know he did, and we have—twice now. Yet still they keep turning back up. You know what I could do?"

"What?" asked Hernanie uneasily.

"I could take these back to Columbia next time I go home, and I could sell them to a dealer in Bogota. There are dozens of emerald dealers there. They would be easy to sell."

"We can't do that! Father said not to. You know how mad he would get if we disobeyed him."

"Who'd tell him—you, me or this corpse?"

"He'd find out somehow."

"No, he wouldn't. How could he? And anyway, Hernanie, the only reason your father didn't want to sell the stones in the first place was because he didn't want this ranch invaded by hundreds of *garimpeiros*: it would screw up our entire operation. But if I sold them in Columbia, no one would know. It's perfect."

"No, it's not. It stinks. If Father ever found out he would kill us."

"But he can't find out, Hernanie. How could he? And anyway, don't you need the cash? I know you. You'll be down in Paraguay gambling again as soon as you have the chance, and you'll lose like you always do and will be forced to ask your Father to bail you out again. Remember how pleasant he was the last time? Remember how he beat the living hell out of you and told you not to ever get in anymore trouble, especially now that you're going to be the son of the president?

"Remember? I remember, and I don't even want to think about what he'll do to you next time. It could hurt him politically if the press got hold of the fact that you were into the Paraguayan Mafia for a couple hundred thousand dollars of bad gambling debts. Wouldn't you like to have some money of your own to blow?"

Hernanie didn't answer.

José looked to Jack and asked, "Hey *gringo*, how much are these emeralds worth?"

Jack rubbed his aching chin in thought. "Well, the big one that the senator kept is worth an easy million. Those aren't worth that much," he lied, "but you might be able to get fifty grand for them."

"Fifty grand? Is that all? You're kidding."

"I wish I was. No, by the time those are faceted, you won't have much. The big ones though, are worth much more."

"What big ones?"

"The other big emeralds that I left in the mine."

"You mean there are others buried in the mine just like the one the senator kept?"

"That's right. Four more just like it."

Hernanie jumped loudly into the conversation, "Then you better show them to us, *gringo*!"

"Why should I?"

Hernanie shouldered his rifle and answered, "Because if you don't, I'm going to kill you."

"You're going to kill me anyway, so go right on ahead. Get it over with, you pussy. Go on, pull the trigger. Pull it!" he shouted. "But if you do, you won't get the other emeralds."

Fonseca's son shook with anger and with greed. He wanted to splatter Jack's brains all over the back of the pickup. He wanted to cut Jack's belly open with a dozen rounds, then watch him try to put his guts back in as he bled to death, moaning and spitting up blood.

But then again, José was right: a couple million of his own would certainly ease the tension between himself and his father. His dad was always generous, but it was never enough. Hernanie couldn't quit the cards once he started losing, and he'd lost a lot—too much, way too much. But with a couple of million as his stake, he could win it all back.

"All right then, if you tell us where the stones are, we won't kill you."

"Just like you didn't kill those three other guys?"

"That's different. They didn't have the other emeralds."

"So what you're telling me is that you'll let me walk out of here, if I show you the other stones?"

"That's right."

"Why should I believe you?"

"I'll give you my word as a Fonseca."

"Your word? I'm afraid I need a little more than that, and not just one of your father's campaign T-shirts either. I'll tell you what. I want you to drive me to the fence and give me a gun, so I can defend myself in case you try to shoot me. Then once I feel safe, I'll draw you a map of where to find the stones."

"A map?"

Hernanie's brows furrowed as he considered the proposition.

José broke his concentration and shattered Jack's hopes with a laugh, a deep belly laugh that rose into hearty humor.

"What's so funny?" asked Hernanie angrily.

"You are!"

"Why?"

"He doesn't have any more emeralds. If he did, he wouldn't have left them in the mine."

"Sure I do," said Jack, knowing the chance was lost.

"I left them there because it was too risky to take them all out at once. I planned to come back with an army of miners once I'd sold those. I was going to invade this place, so once we started digging, the word would already have been out, and you wouldn't have been able to stop us. But

I'm willing to trade the emeralds now. Take it all. All I want is my life."

José, who was still laughing, asked, "And what about your girlfriend?"

"You can keep her. I'll get another one. I just want to live."

"Well, sorry about that, *amigo*, but we can't let that happen." His laughter fell to smiles. "I'd like to let you go, though. You deserve it. You really had Hernanie going. He almost gave you his gun!"

José laughed again.

"*Mentira!*" shouted an angry Hernanie, who let loose a volley of machine gun fire just above Jack's head.

Jack dropped to the bed of the truck, watching to see what would happen next.

José grabbed Hernanie's gun by the stock. "Better save those, in case we need them. Wait until we get to the mine. If you shoot him now, we'll have to dig the hole. Let him do the work."

"No, I'm not going to shoot him, though I'd like to. It will be better to know that he's dying slowly in the mine like the rest of them did, clawing in the dirt like a rat."

"Except that son of a mother who bit me," added José as he massaged his shoulder. "Next time I meet a *zagaiero*, I'll kill him out of principle."

"Good idea. And next time I meet an American, I'll put a bullet through his head!"

"Easy, *patrão*. You're going to be living in the *Palácio da Alvorada*, and your house will be full of American officials. Take advantage of their daughters, but don't shoot them— that's bad for your father's image."

"Yeah, that's what I'll do. I'll screw their daughters," scoffed Hernanie as he pointed his rifle at Jack and feigned pulling the trigger. "And every time I cum, I'll think back to this asshole and putting a bullet in his head."

"That's it, Hernanie," said José.

He looked ahead as the truck slowed down. "Look. We're almost at the mine."

Hernanie and Jack both twisted to get a better view around the cab. Up in front, outlined by floodlights mounted on the truck's roll bar, were familiar landmarks. Jack knew his time was near, and though prayer wasn't habitual for him, he prayed that he would be able to somehow survive this so he could save Marisa. Nothing else cluttered his mind. Nothing else mattered. What could he do?

The truck pulled to a stop as it neared the trees covering the low hill.

"Get out," said José, now all business.

Jack did as he was told, and they all walked to the mine. All were unencumbered except for rifles, other than the driver who lugged a cooler. When they got to the filled-in mineshaft, José picked up Jack's shovel from where he'd left it and tossed it to him.

"Dig," he commanded, and Jack did, though slowly.

Jack pondered his options, said more prayers and watched his captors for an opening. The rest of them busied themselves with beer drinking and laughter.

Hernanie and the driver got drunk in a hurry, Jack noticed, while José, who drank with them, seemed to pace himself enough to keep his wits about him. Jack knew that if a bullet were to kill him, it would be one of José's. The other two were smug and ridiculous, too wrapped up in their drinking to take much notice of the man a few feet away who would shoot them in a second if given just a chance.

While he dug, they drank on, seemingly unaware of the situation, like revelers at an Irish wake. He thought of

Marisa and wondered what would happen to her. She might be dead already, he thought sadly, but then considering her beauty, he realized they might keep her alive a long time. He shuddered at the thought of her being used by men like these.

If only there were a way. Prayer had never been much a part of his nature, but he prayed as he dug. He prayed for justice and just one opening, just one second, just one meter of even ground. Then if he died, he would know that he died trying.

He dug on while their merriment continued. It was interrupted by the stench of Heiner as he began to dig him up for the second time. He looked sadly at his friend and hoped desperately that they wouldn't be reunited soon. The German was almost a brother, a rival sibling who always came out ahead, but even so, he didn't want to be eternal roommates.

"What's that awful stink?" queried Hernanie from above.

"It's a body, asshole," answered Jack. "Why don't you give me a hand with it? It's heavy."

"Deal with it yourself, *gringo*, or I'll shoot your balls off." Hernanie laughed at the thought, but then the stench struck his nostrils and caught him up short. He began to feel queasy.

"Listen," he said to the other two, "You watch this pile of shit. I've got to take a piss."

"Me too," seconded the driver.

"Watch him, José. We'll be back in a second."

José nodded. Jack dug the earth from beneath his friends armpits and said quietly, "Sorry Heiner, I don't want to have to keep disturbing you."

Then he thought back to the old days when Heiner once cleaned out a bar after a local took a cheap shot at his American friend. *I wish you could help me now*, he lamented.

"Can't you give me a hand with this?" asked Jack up to José.

"Sorry, *amigo*. I would, but I'd smell like that all night and would have to throw away my clothes. It shouldn't make a difference to you. You'll smell like that in a day or two, anyway."

Jack grabbed Heiner under the arms and tugged him free of the entrance, then fell back with the corpse atop of him. He started to gag and realized that he might be able to use the gag reflex to aid him. A plan—a long shot—formed. It would probably get him killed, but what the hell? He was already headed that way.

Jack held in his bile, then threw his shovel up and out of the hole. He knew he had to act fast, so he took a deep breath. He grappled the body and managed to scramble out of the hole with it. When he made the surface, he dropped it right on the silver tips of José's boots.

The Colombian was overwhelmed by the rotten smell of death and stepped back, wiping at his face as if it could clear his nostrils. Jack took the moment of confusion to duck down, pick up his shovel and bat José full in the face with a major league crack.

The Colombian screamed as he fell backward, and it was almost Jack's undoing. The other two men heard the sound, and drunk or not, they reacted quickly. José's rifle sailed wide when he was hit, and Jack chased after it. Before he could reach it, the night came alive with machine gun fire, and the ground near him erupted with a line of puffs.

Lacking any other cover, Jack dove back into the hole, then peered out of it—the other two were running toward him, guns blazing. Just as he headed down the shaft, he spied the bag that José dropped when he fell. Jack grabbed it, and then like Alice, down the rabbit hole he went.

He scrambled through the narrow tunnel as fast as humanly possible, until he sprawled into the horizontal shaft. Once there, he moved to the side, then stopped for a moment to think. Bullets rained down the tunnel to sink themselves in the talc beyond him. With a mental coin-toss he ran right a few feet and then squatted, waiting.

"Mother fucker! Mother fucker!" screamed Hernanie above the mine entrance as he changed clips. "The mother fucker, knocked José out and got away from us!"

"Well," the driver replied, "Why don't we just bury him then and go home?"

"No!" he screamed. "I told Father that we would find that other body, and I need those emeralds!"

Hernanie stepped over to check José, hoping he could help. But he was unconscious—his face mashed in a bloody caricature of what it used to be. José was out of the picture.

"*Merda!*" screamed Hernanie. "Shit! Shit! Shit! We'll have to go in and get him by ourselves. But listen, shoot him if you have to, but don't kill him. I'm going to feed that bastard his own balls before he dies! Let's go. You first."

The driver did as he was told and reluctantly crawled down the shaft. Hernanie followed close after, and in his excitement and anger, he totally forgot about flashlights. At the end of the tunnel, they climbed out into the horizontal shaft and stood.

As soon as the driver asked Hernanie, "What next?" they heard a sound to the left. With a yell, the driver opened up and fired at the sound while running toward it. His charge ended in a long scream that lasted for four seconds before it died in a muffled thump. He had chased the ricochet of a well-thrown stone to his death in the pit below.

Hernanie followed him initially, then stood still, awaiting word from the driver. Soon after his scream died out, Hernanie decided that Jack must have grabbed him, so he let out a volley in the dark, hoping to hit the *gringo*. But he shot in the wrong direction, and Jack used the cover of the sound and the light of his shots to close-in on him and brain him with a rock.

The senator's son fell like a rag doll, button-eyed and boneless . Jack disarmed him, searched him, then dragged him slowly to the surface. Once they reached fresh air, Hernanie still a toy, Jack edged his weapon out of the hole and looked up over the edge. José was just coming to. He was on his knees, breathing deep, trying to regain his senses. Jack didn't give him the chance. He leaped up, rushed to the Colombian and kicked him hard in the back of the head. José fell inert to the ground while Jack panted above him with his rifle shouldered and ready to put a quick end to any fight. There wasn't any. José was out again, cold.

Jack backed away to the shaft where he had left Hernanie, who was just beginning to come awake. When his eyes fluttered open with a moan, Jack fired a shot that just cleared his nose to get his attention.

Hernanie fell back, screaming, "No! No! Please don't kill me! My father's rich, and he will pay!"

"Why the fuck would he pay for you?" asked Jack, doubting that he could put up with a son like this himself, but hoping the senator would.

"He'll pay! He'll pay! I promise!"

"I've heard that before, asshole. Where's the proof?"

"He'll pay you—I promise!"

"I said, I've heard that."

"Please, I promise!"

"I don't care about promises. I've already heard your promises, *canalha*. I need something that I can use— something that can get me out of this nightmare."

"I can help!"

"How?"

"I'll ask my father to let you go."

Jack growled and fired a short burst into the loam above Hernanie's head.

"I'll force him to let you go! Please! Don't kill me!"

"How are you going to force him to let me go?" asked Jack with growing interest.

"I'll tell you about our business, then he'll have to listen to you."

"What business?"

"Our cocaine business. I'll tell you everything, but please don't kill me."

"Well, we'll see how it goes. Now get the fuck up and drive me to your ranch house."

"Sure. Sure," said Hernanie as he climbed out of the hole and headed to the truck, arms up, hands pointed to the sky.

Chapter Nine

Senator Fonseca was sitting in his darkened living room in a deep leather chair, wearing only briefs. Election news blazed from the TV in an eerie blue glow that paled the senator's large and hairy belly, and glinted off the ice cubes in his whiskey like moon shadows on a tide.

He turned when he heard the door open and said, "Hernanie, is that you?"

Hernanie cringed at the poke of the rifle barrel on his neck and answered, "Yes, Father. It's me."

Jack prodded him into the room, and they slowly approached the senator who had turned back to watch the latest polls.

He spoke as graphs rolled along the screen, "Good. I'm glad you're back. I broke that little filly for you. She was feisty at first, but I took the fire out of her quick enough. I think you'll find her an easy ride. She's all yours if you want her. Just get her out of my bedroom, son, and call the maid and have her change my sheets. Make sure you get the little slut out of the house and taken care of first thing in morning. I don't want to see her when I wake up."

"You won't have to," said a voice that was not his son's.

Hernanie stumbled forward with the force of Jack's kick and stood before the television trembling.

Fonseca rose. He looked first at his son and then into the shadows.

"You?"

"That's right. Where is she?"

Fonseca stared into the barrel of the rifle in disbelief.

"I said, where is she!"

"In my bedroom."

"Show me."

Fonseca led them to his bedroom door, then stopped.

"Open it."

Fonseca hesitated, then slowly did as he was ordered. The door swung open to reveal Marisa tied spread eagle on a large four-poster bed, staring up to the ceiling in shock. Jack pushed the men into the room, then hit them both hard in the kidneys with his rifle butt. They fell to the floor, breathless from the pain, temporarily incapacitated. Jack rushed past them to the girl. He looked down at her and was horrified by what he saw.

Her face was puffy with bruises. Blood, now dried, had coursed from her nostrils and from her cracked lip. One of her eyes had already begun to purple, and there was blood between her legs.

Jack grabbed a blanket and threw it over her naked form, then he quickly untied her. She didn't move as he worked, and she didn't even look at him. Her eyes stayed fixed on the ceiling. Jack hugged her to him and kissed her on the forehead.

"It's all right, Marisa. I'm here now. It's all right."

He hugged her and soothed her until she eventually looked at him. With recognition came tears. She sobbed into him wildly and clung to him. Jack was overcome with grief and guilt for letting this happen, and was also filled with animal rage and the desire to kill. As Marisa cried, the

Fonsecas began to stir. The senator raised himself up onto his hands and knees.

"If you make another move, I'm going to shoot you," said Jack with steel in his voice.

"Both of you lie face-down on the floor with your hands behind your heads. If you move or say a single word, I will kill you both. Understand?"

They nodded and did as they were told.

Jack stroked Marisa's hair and comforted her for a long moment. "Listen to me, *querida*. We have to get out of here as quick as we can. But first I want you to take a shower. Get cleaned up. Wash away all the blood and all the evil. I won't let him hurt you again, okay?"

She nodded. Then he stood her up and pointed her to the open door of a bathroom. She walked in, shutting the door behind her.

Jack looked down at the men on the floor and wanted to kill them. He wanted to beat them to death with his own hands and to paint the walls red with their blood. That's what he wanted to do, but he knew it wasn't wise. *No*, if he shot them it might raise an alarm, bringing who knew how many armed thugs down upon him. And even if they managed to get off the ranch without detection, he doubted they could get out of the state, much less the country. Fonseca would surely be found the next morning, and that would spark a national manhunt.

He stared down at them as they lay there on the floor. The senator, naked except for the patch of black fabric stretched tight over his wide ass, looked like some type of vile walrus loafing on the beach. Hernanie lay beside him and cowered like a whipped puppy. They seemed pathetic, but they weren't. They were vicious rapists and murderers. The best thing for the world, Jack thought, would have been to pump them full of bullets, but he couldn't do it. He needed them alive to insure his and Marisa's safety.

He needed a hostage. But which one? Kidnapping the senator was a bad idea. As soon as the kidnapping was discovered, they would have not only the senator's thugs after them, but also the forces of the entire country. What if he kidnapped the senator's son? They could drive out of the ranch with him and no one would suspect a thing. Then they could catch an airplane to Rio, and from there, grab a connection to Miami. The senator was too much in the spotlight, but his son wasn't. These rich, young Brazilians flew all over the world. It might just work.

But then what? Would they ever be safe again? Probably not.

Jack thought back over all he'd learned on the drive back from the mine. Hernanie was a font of information when you stuck a gun in his ear. He explained everything in the hour and a half it took them to get back. He now knew the senator was using the ranch as an entry point for Colombian cocaine smuggled in through the Chaco desert in Bolivia, then boated or flown through the Pantanal, depending on the season.

From there, the drugs were smuggled in false-bottomed cattle trucks to a farmer's cooperative on the other side of Cuiabá, where they were sealed in soybean sacks or drums of soybean oil. The drugs in oil were then shipped to buyers in either Europe or America, while those in sacks were sent to Rio and São Paulo for domestic consumption.

It was a big operation with a distribution network in five countries and a twenty percent stake of the Brazilian market, all computerized and run from the senator's isolated ranch house. The methods had been faultless until they caught The Professor and the string of prospectors that followed in his steps. Word of a producing emerald mine would bring a thousand *garimpeiros* in a week, and with miners would come the law, both to keep the miners from killing each other and to see that the government got its share. It would have ruined everything. That's why all the murders happened.

The sounds of the shower died, and he could hear Marisa opening the curtain through the bathroom door. He walked over to Hernanie and stuck his rifle barrel in the back of his neck.

"Go get her some clothes." He looked around the room and saw several family portraits, smiling pictures of the famous senator, his lovely wife, Hernanie, a younger boy and a pretty daughter who looked the same age as Marisa. He looked at the pictures. There was one of the proud father hugging his daughter on her fifteenth birthday. Had he beaten and raped another girl like her when he left the party, Jack wondered? He felt ill. What drove a man like Fonseca? He dug the barrel harder into Hernanie's flesh.

"Now, go get some of your sister's clothes, something pretty and comfortable to travel in, and bring them back here quickly. If you try to call anyone or if you go for a gun, I'm going to kill you and your father. I'll kill you slowly. Do you understand?"

"Yes," whimpered Hernanie. "Yes, I'll do just as you say."

"If you don't, you're a dead man, and your brother and sister will be fatherless." He prodded him harder. "Now go. Quickly!"

Hernanie scrambled to his feet and ran from the room. Jack moved away from the door, so he had a clear line of fire should Hernanie try anything. He listened to the son rummage through drawers in another room. Hernanie returned in a few minutes with a bundle of clothes that shook in his hands.

"Set them by the bathroom door, then lie down by your father."

He did as he was told.

Jack knocked on the bathroom door and said softly, "Marisa, I have some clothes for you to wear. You can open the door and get them. I won't look." He stepped away from the door and heard it open and close behind him.

"Get up, senator, and lie down on your bed."

Fonseca rose, hate glinting in the darkness of his eyes. He walked slowly over to the bed and laid down, watching Jack as he went.

"You'll never get away with this, you know," he said.

"Shut up."

Jack called to Hernanie. "Tie your father just like he tied up the girl."

Hernanie hesitated.

"Do it!" Jack shouldered his rifle and pointed it at the senator's head. The son then scooted over and took his father's wrist. The senator sat up and resisted him. Their eyes met. The hate that Jack saw was still there, but intensified and harsher. Hernanie quailed under the look and wavered.

"I told you to tie him up, not to hold his hand." Jack prodded him, and he began trussing up his father. The senator lay soft and flaccid, inert in aspect but for the flames that flickered in his eyes, a fire of vengeance and evil. He glared at his son, who cowered and looked away as he fumbled with the ropes.

"Tie him, tightly! I don't want him out of bed until morning."

Then Jack turned his ire to the senator.

"Fonseca, I know all about your operation here and why you didn't want the Borba mine exploited, but why everything else? You have all this country has to offer. Why run drugs? Why murder? Why rape? It makes no sense. You are a perverse and evil man, you bastard. Why? Everything in the world has been given you, yet you take away the lives of others. Why?"

Fonseca glared venomously at him, but didn't answer. Why should he bother to answer this American, this robber on his lands? Why should he try to explain to this chattel, this foreign invader, that his birthright sprung from a captaincy chartered by the King of Portugal himself three hundred years before. His ancestors had battled their way a thousand miles from the coast, fighting Indians all the way, for the glory of God and for Portugal, and they were justly rewarded for their services. They were lords of the land for perpetuity. But now his birthright was endangered, and he'd had to fight to maintain it all his life.

Pressure from within, pressure from without. It was a constant struggle for people of his class. The emerging middle class was always clamoring for a better standard of living, more and greater opportunities, a bigger voice in government, a bigger share of the pie. Well, why should they have more? They had it too good as it was. Was it their ancestors who were deeded the land? What rights did they have to anything? None. They were nothing but servants to the ancient families of power.

They were servants, little more than slaves—most of them had nigger or Indian blood in them anyway, yet they presumed to ask for equality and power, thought the senator. Never! He had ways of dealing with unruly peons on his *fazendas*. He wished that national government were so easy, but it wasn't. That's what the drugs were for.

It was nothing new, nothing much different than what the British did in China with opium. Drugs were power, a tool, simple and effective. He was draining the will of the fractious masses, undermining their resolve, turning their youth into tractable addicts, turning their cities to violence, and they were paying him dearly for it. It was beautiful. Who had time to protest for land reform when they were busy all night breaking into neighbors' houses, scraping up money for a fix?

But the real beauty of it all was that he was subtly striking back at the heavy-handed, intrusive Americans who were hellbent on turning every other country on earth into a copy of Ohio. Fuck them and their worker's paradise. He'd been to Ohio, and he didn't like it. Fuck them and their democracy. What was democracy anyway? Government by the masses, government by the ignorant, that's all it was, like trying to run a farm by giving it over to the pigs.

And look at who ran America—that bunch of striped-pants faggots who had been courting him since his rise in the polls didn't seem very impressive to him. How they cooed and slavered when he conceded to their growing list of constant demands. Fools, did they really hope to rule the next president of Brazil? Maybe *they* were on drugs.

He smiled when he thought of the meeting he'd had with the ambassador and DEA officials the previous month, when he pledged closer cooperation in the effort to stop drug smuggling. It was all he could do not to laugh in their serious, stony faces.

If he wasn't so full of hate, he might laugh now. But he couldn't, not now, not after having been betrayed by his eldest son. Hernanie had been weak and worthless all his life. He couldn't be trusted to finish college. How could he be trusted to run their empire? Fonseca was disgusted watching his son tie the knots, hunched over and cowering like a cur. He felt nothing of fatherly love. He felt betrayal and loathing. Hernanie wasn't worthy to bear the Fonseca name. He couldn't be trusted with anything. Would Afonso Fonseca dared to have tied his father? No. He would have died first, but not Hernanie. He was a disgrace to the family and a coward. What was he to do with him?

When Hernanie was finished tying his father, Jack motioned him back and checked the knots by pulling them roughly, enough to make the senator wince. They were all tight.

Jack asked Hernanie, "You said that your cocaine operation is all run from here by computer. Is that true?"

Hernanie stared at his feet when he answered to avoid his father's glare.

"Yes," he said meekly.

"Show me."

Jack threw a blanket over the senator, and it covered him completely, head and all. Then he opened the bathroom door and led Marisa past him and out the door, with Hernanie leading the way.

Hernanie took them to the computer where his father was working earlier.

"Turn it on and get into your business files."

"I don't know how," he stammered .

"You'd better." Jack cuffed him and pushed him down into the chair.

A dazed Hernanie started the machine and was soon rolling through dozens of files all stored on the computer's C drive.

"Open a file."

"Which one?"

"That one."

Jack pointed to a file labeled, C:\DIST\BRASIL. Hernanie pressed enter, and a dozen business addresses, phone numbers and delivery dates glowed from the screen. The addresses were in every major Brazilian city.

"Try this one." He pointed at another file, labeled C:\FINANCE\ACCTS_PANAMA. It was a list of nameless, numbered bank accounts and the amounts they contained. Jack glanced at it quickly, but he was sure that they were worth tens of millions of dollars.

"Now this one." A file named C:\DIST\EUA_SUL contained a list of a dozen addresses and numbers in Texas and Florida, with a list of both past and future dates attached to each.

It was shocking and was certainly enough to condemn the senator to several lifetimes in prison on two continents. An idea began to form.

"Marisa, do you have a passport?" he asked. "Marisa?"

He shook her gently to bring her back from wherever she was.

"*Querida,* do you and your mom have passports?"

"Yes. We all got passports when *Papai* came back from Rio. *Mamãe* was excited. She wanted to go to Paris."

"Good. Maybe she'll get there yet."

Jack looked the machine over and saw that it had a tape drive, which had the capacity to hold thousands of pages of information.

"Copy it to tape."

"What?"

"All of it. Everything in memory, except games. Copy it all. Make me two copies. Go on, get going!"

After a warning nudge, Hernanie started copying and after 40 long and nervous minutes, Jack had Fonseca's entire operation in the palm of his hand. He motioned Hernanie to lead them back to the bedroom. At the door of the master bedroom, Jack combed Marisa's hair lightly back and said, "Wait right here, *querida*. I'll just be a minute."

She nodded, but shook as she did so, hugging herself and staring to the floor. He thrust his hostage ahead of him into the room where he jerked off the blanket, exposing the fat and fuming senator, splayed out like a skydiving flasher who'd left his raincoat in the plane.

"We're leaving now," said Jack. "And you are going to help us."

The senator studied him darkly and then asked, "Help you, you *miserável*—I'd rather die!"

"Easily arranged."

Jack pressed his rifle barrel roughly into the senator's black-clad crotch. Fonseca groaned in pain.

"Don't tempt me, asshole. Now listen. We're going to drive out of here tonight and nobody's going to stop us. Not now, not when we fly out of Cuiabá and not when we fly out of the country. You're an important senator. You said the American ambassador is a friend of yours, didn't you?"

Fonseca didn't answer.

"Didn't you?"

Questioning steel pressured his balls and brought a strong response.

"YES!"

"Good. That's the spirit. I want you to call the ambassador and arrange emergency medical visas for Isabella Fontes and her daughter, Marisa. She has cancer and needs to go to the M.D. Anderson hospital in Texas for treatment. Got it?"

Again came the pressure. Harder this time.

"GOT IT!"

"Good. You also need a visa for your son, Hernanie, who will accompany them."

The ashen senator nodded his head while staring at his son with unconcealed rage.

"I'm sorry, father. He'll kill us all. He killed José and Donaldo."

"Shut up," said Jack.

The senator only stared.

"And senator, I know you want to murder us now and will want to later once we're in the U.S., but it is not in your best interest."

The senator turned away from his son and looked questioningly up to his captor.

"You see," Jack said. "Your son gave me a copy of all your business transactions, and once I'm in the States, copies of them will go into safe deposit boxes around the country. Should anything happen to me, Marisa or her mother, I'll leave instructions with my lawyers to have these copies made available to the press. If I were you, I'd wish us all good health, senator, because I know you have grand plans. Now make the phone call."

After a nervous search for his father's Rolodex, Hernanie got the number and the senator made the call. The calm in the senator's voice was remarkable to Jack. He was different than his son, who shook as if he expected to be struck as he held the receiver to his father's head. And Hernanie was a different man than the one he'd been just a few short hours before, who had laughed and drank while forcing Jack at gunpoint to dig his own grave.

Once the phone call was made, Jack started to march Hernanie out the door so he could fetch his passport. As Jack turned, he noticed the large emerald crystal the senator had taken from him, set on a dresser below a wedding portrait—young Senhora Fonseca in a billowy gown, held by an innocent-looking young man who had somehow transformed into the monster trussed to the bed. Sins of the father? Fruits of a captive world in which all his wants and lusts were met without reserve? Jack never knew the root or cause of evil, but the seemingly happy house in which he stood was full of it. It dwelled in the hearts of these men.

Well, it wasn't his to understand, he reasoned. It was his to escape and to survive, and it was his to take back what The Professor and Heiner had paid for with their lives. The emerald was Marisa's now. He stepped over to the dresser and pocketed the stone. They left the bound and scowling senator, quickly grabbed his son's passport and were soon on their way.

Hernanie chauffeured them through the gate without a question from the gate guards who waived them through. It was a long way to town on a rutted dirt road, but with the luxury of the big four-wheel drive, they made it in four hours. A quilt of darkness still blanketed Poconé when they rolled through at three a.m. and headed down the farm road that led to Marisa's house.

Chapter Ten

The house was as dark as the night when they pulled up to it and parked in the yard. They all got out and walked to the porch with Marisa in the lead, but Jack stopped her at the open door. Nobody sleeps with their front door open.

Jack pushed Hernanie into the house and followed, the machine gun pressed into his back. As they moved into the shadowed room, he was about to call out for Marisa's mother when Hernanie screamed.

At their feet lay the body of *Senhora* Fontes, mouth agape, stuffed with the green and red feathers of Eduardo, her pet parrot. Jack looked down in horror, his mind spinning to figure out what happened. It must have been Fonseca.

"What is it, Jack?" called Marisa from the door. "What's the matter?"

"*Meu Deus,*" cried Hernanie. "They're going to kill us all!"

"Shut up!"

"What's the matter, Jack?"

"Marisa, stay outside."

How could this have happened? How could he have reacted so fast? Jack didn't have to wait long for an answer. A light clicked on in the corner to reveal José sitting in a chair pointing a pistol at them.

"Oh, let the girl in, *amigo*. It's her mother after all."

He shouted past them, "Come on in, *senhorita*. Come say hello to your mother."

Marisa tentatively stepped through the door, then screamed and flew down to cradle her mother, who was lying between them and José. She grabbed the parrot and struggled to wrench it free, but in dying it had bitten down hard into her mother's tongue and was firmly stuck. With a final tug she freed it, sending the parrot's body and a bloody hunk of tongue across the room. Marisa closed her mother's staring eyes, then rocked her body back and forth, wailing, totally oblivious to the scene playing out above her.

Jack stepped back and brought his rifle up to the back of Hernanie's head, then stared into the eyes of José. His eyes and his silver tipped boots were the only things recognizable about the man. His nose was bent, and his face was swollen from where Jack had caught him with the flat of a shovel. He was a mess, but his eyes were the same, and now they sparkled with the cold anticipation of a quick revenge. Jack couldn't believe he was seeing him.

"How did you get here?"

"I flew. Don't you know that all big ranchers keep planes out here? It's the only way they can keep an eye on their stock. Too bad, if you had known, Hernanie could have flown you to Cuiabá himself. He's a pilot, aren't you Hernanie?"

Hernanie didn't answer, but began to shake again.

"How did you get back from the mine?" questioned Jack.

"By a bit of good luck: one of our fence patrols passed by and picked me up. We rushed straight back to the ranch house and only missed you by about twenty minutes. Some of our boys should be here shortly. They left by truck about half an hour after you. I worried about them. I was afraid they might catch up with you before I did and deny me the pleasure of killing you myself."

"Don't even think about it. You try anything, and I'll blow his head off."

A shot rang out. Hernanie screamed and clutched his belly, then he fell to the ground and started moaning loudly.

José smiled and said, "You don't have to bother yourself about that. I was asked to save you the trouble."

He spoke down to Hernanie while keeping his eyes and his pistol trained on Jack. "Your father wasn't pleased with your betrayal, Hernanie. I guess he finally gave up on you and your continuous troublemaking, so he asked me to take care of you. I could have gone for a head or a chest shot, but you've been quite a little pain in the ass over the years, so this seemed more appropriate. You know you could last a day like that. I think it gets worse over time."

Hernanie groaned louder. José's smile broadened.

"Two down and two to go," he said. "Hernanie was fun. So was that woman. I would have just shot her, but she wouldn't shut up. She and that bird wouldn't stop squawking, so I decided to let them squawk at each other for a while. It was giving me a headache, but it looks as if they're all squawked out now. Hernanie's groans don't bother me, though. They're music to my ears." He focused fully on Jack. "Now what am I going to do with you?"

"You do anything, and I'll spray you. Even if you shoot me, I'll still pull the trigger." Jack's finger tightened on the trigger of the machine gun. "Do you think it's worth the risk?"

José pondered the question while watching through his pistol sight, which was aimed at Jack's head. If he got him in the brain, he might not be able to fire, but then again he might. It wasn't worth it. There would be another chance. He said nothing, just watched and waited.

They held each other in their sights until Jack finally spoke, "Come on, Marisa, let's get out of here."

"No! I can't leave my mother."

"We have to, *querida.* There's nothing we can do here, and other men will be here soon. If we don't leave now, they'll kill us."

"No."

"Marisa! Come on. We have to go! Crawl until you get behind me. Then go out and start the truck. I'll come out when I hear the engine."

She didn't move.

"Please, Marisa, they'll kill us if we stay here. We've got to beat them. We've got to live. Alive, we can avenge your parents. Dead, we can't."

She laid her mother's body gently down, then crawled away below the line of fire. Soon after, the Range Rover came to life. When Jack heard it, he began to back out slowly, ready to shoot, his eyes on José's, watching for the telltale movement of action.

Adrenaline pumped throughout his whole body, and the short walk backward to the truck seemed an eternity. But he made it, and José didn't try to follow him out the door. He climbed in the passenger seat without turning around and faced backward with his rifle pointed toward the door. "Drive us out of town, Marisa."

As soon as she began to pull away, José started shooting from a window and shattered their back windshield.

"Go!"

She sped down the road while Jack returned fire, spraying her house with bullets. He quit firing when his gun was empty. They were now unarmed.

She turned toward Poconé, and they were soon roaring down the *avenida principal* toward the road that led to

Cuiabá. They didn't get far before they saw a roadblock up ahead.

"Quick! Turn off here before they see us."

Marisa turned off the pavement into a warren of residential streets, which she backtracked through until they came to wider dirt road. "This is the way to Bolivia," she said. "The border's about three hundred kilometers from here."

"Let's go."

She pulled out onto the road and they drove out of town. A few minutes later, they rounded a bend and nearly crashed into the police cars that blocked their path.

Marisa slammed the brakes, spinning them half-way around. Without having to reverse, she floored the gas pedal and raced toward town. Both police cars were soon in hot pursuit. They wove their way through the village, but couldn't dislodge their tail. Finally in desperation, Marisa gunned the Range Rover down a rutted track that was worse than all the rest they'd four-wheeled over.

"Where are we going, Marisa? Is this a way out of town?"

"It will get us out of town, but not much further."

"Where are we going?"

"Back into the Pantanal."

They were headed down the *Transpantaneira*, a raised dirt road started twenty years before in a grand attempt to open the Pantanal for habitation and commerce by linking Poconé with the city of Corumbá three hundred and forty kilometers to the south, but like many projects started in Brazil, it was not yet half-finished and ended at a fishing camp on the bank of the Rio Cuiabá about two hundred kilometers short of its planned destination.

"We can steal a boat and maybe get to Paraguay or Bolivia," Marisa said. "I don't know what I'll do from there." She started to cry.

"It'll be all right, Marisa. I'll take care of you. Let's just get away from the police."

He looked back and could see the flashing red lights of the police cars behind them. It seemed as if they were gaining ground, pushing their little cars to the limit.

"I'll lose them. You can't drive a car like that on this road. It gets worse the further you go."

She drove on. Up ahead was a rickety, one-lane wooden bridge like the one he'd driven across to get to her house. He cringed as they bumped up over it at full throttle, with the sound of boards cracking beneath them.

"Are there many bridges like that, Marisa?"

"Over a hundred, but most aren't in that good of shape. A few got washed out last year and haven't been fixed yet, but don't worry: I know which ones. *Papai* and I panned for gold down here last December—just before we found the Borba mine."

Still more tears welled with the thought, but she didn't have time to dwell on it.

They could hear pistols firing behind them. She stepped on the gas while Jack fastened his seat belt and hunched down, expecting a crash or a bullet. Young Brazilians behind the wheel of an automobile sometimes become Ayrton Senna incarnate—the spirit of Formula One dwells in most—and Marisa was not an exception.

She blew down the raised dirt road as if she were on the circuit in Monaco, just a lap shy of the checkered flag, and the police who followed her didn't seem to want to settle for second place. It was a race that defied logic, even in crisis. She was driving way too fast, but it paid off, for soon there was only one bubble gum machine flashing behind them. One of the police cars was down; though why, they would never know—probably a broken axle.

The other car kept on coming. That's when Marisa's knowledge of the road really paid off. For the first thirty kilometers or so, they had to duck down and dodge bullets, but after that the police either tired of shooting or had run low on ammunition. Then it was a more relaxed, though bone-shaking chase.

At kilometer fifty, Marisa nearly lost it when she hit a crossing caiman, but she regained control quickly and drove on. She was counting the bridges now and was carefully watching for landmarks that flashed by as they rumbled on. This was it, the bridge at kilometer 80.

"Hold on, Jack," she said as she geared down hard, killed the lights and headed off the road, just as they were about to cross over yet another wooden bridge. She let the truck bump and roll to a stop in a field while the headlights of the police car flashed past them down the road.

"What are you doing?" asked her jarred and startled companion.

"Bridge is out. Those guys are about to find out."

They heard a skid and a crash in the distance.

Moments after the crash, they heard faint screaming.

"That hole must be full of caiman," said Jack absently. Marisa looked away, out her window a moment before starting the car to drive slowly through the pasture, around the pond and back up onto the road. Once she gained the road, she drove more slowly.

"We'll be safe for now," she explained. "And we'll make it to Porto Jofre before daylight, so we can steal a fishing boat. Once we're on the water, we'll be okay. They'll never find us then."

She drove on into the night.

Chapter Eleven

A s they neared the fishing camp of Porto Jofre, Marisa extinguished her headlights and pulled to a stop. It was around 4 a.m., a little more than an hour before sunrise. They needed to move fast.

They checked the truck for any useful gear and found two rods and reels, a flashlight and a shovel. Jack left the empty and ineffectual machine gun in his seat, rolled down the windows, then strained to push the truck down the bank and into the river where it sank like just another submerging caiman.

As the Range Rover disappeared beneath the muddy water, they walked quietly past the four stilted houses that comprised the camp and onto the dock where they began inspecting boats.

There were several of the roughly built and brightly painted longboats common to the area, most powered only by oars, but also a few with motors. They chose one with a 45 horsepower Johnson outboard, the most powerful of the lot. They increased its range and slowed any pursuers by robbing the other four motored boats of their gas tanks. They had nearly twenty gallons of fuel, which was good: they would need it, as this was the last gas stop for over three hundred kilometers.

Once they had the tanks in place in the bilges, Jack untied the boat and pushed them off. They paddled downstream with the current, until they were well past possible hearing range, then he cranked the engine and they motored away as quickly as they could. There were sure to be boats out searching for them soon, possibly as early as that morning. None of the boats at the camp could catch up with them, though, not unless they had extra gas tanks. They both hoped that it would buy them time.

Marisa knew the river well and maneuvered through the darkness while Jack sat in the bow and watched for signs of other boats ahead. Porto Jofre was long behind them when the sun began to rise above the bird-flowered treetops, making them plainly visible to anyone else on the river or to any passing airplane.

They killed the engine, pulled it up so that their draft was only a few inches, then paddled into a narrow, snaky creek that was shadowed from above by a green and purple canopy of *jenipapo* and *piuva* trees, and which was hidden from the river by its many bends. Jack tied the painter to the trunk of a thin *acuri* palm, then they lay down to sleep, curled up between the thwarts of their boat. It had been an eternal night, and they were both exhausted.

Jack awoke to noises. One was the too-near idle of an outboard, somewhere close on the river, and the other was moaning and thrashing—it was Marisa caught in the grip of a nightmare.

He shook her awake, and she woke up screaming. His hands moved quickly to stifle her screams and calm her, but she resisted at first, squirming wildly in his grip until she calmed with recognition. Jack held a finger to his lips then released his grip. They both crouched in silence, listening to the boat, hoping that it would soon pass on and that it wasn't searching for them. Eventually its droning fell to nothing. There was silence on the river.

"What time is it?" asked Marisa as she pushed herself up from the bottom of the boat.

"Almost five. We've been asleep for nine hours."

"I could sleep for a year. I'm exhausted."

"I know you are, *querida*. You can sleep a little longer if you want. It won't be dark for another two hours, so we can't move for a while. I'll catch us some fish while you take a nap. We need to eat something. We haven't had anything for over a day and a half."

She nodded, then lay down in the bilges and was soon back asleep, jumping through the torture of her dreams. Jack's heart broke to see her balled up in the fetal position, tears running even as she slept. But there was little he could do for her.

Bruises puffed and painted ugly reminders across her face, and he wished that he had killed the senator. Sparing his life hadn't brought them anything, and now the bastard was probably directing their manhunt personally. Jack pulsed with rage and wished he had a chance to live the last day over.

He got up, stepped ashore and collected a handful of ripe *jenipapo* berries for bait. Then he fished. In less than an hour he landed two pacu, both around a pound. It was dinner aplenty, but he wished they had something other than fish to eat. The novelty of living off the land had left him. He longed for a hamburger. *Oh well, at least they were still alive to eat*, something that seemed miracle enough as he thought back over the past 24 hours. He hoped more miracles would come their way in the future. They would need them. He prayed for deliverance as he filleted and de-scaled their dinner.

He laid the fillets out on a palm frond, chucked the gutted remains into the water ahead of the boat, then climbed aboard to search for the box of matches he had seen in the clutter of the bow. As he searched through the empty cans and assorted other junk, he heard strange chirps and high-pitched growls just ahead of the prow.

Startled, he looked up to find himself face to face with the largest otter he had ever seen. Judging from the size of its head and paws, it was easily five feet long. It watched him, unconcerned, as it ravaged a skeletal fish like a piece of corn-on-the-cob. Then it dove into the water and came up with the other. Jack laughed out loud at the antics of the glandular otter, and wanted to reach out and pet it.

"Be careful," warned Marisa, who had woken with his laughter. "*Ariranhas* are dangerous. They can kill a man."

"Otters don't kill people. That's ridiculous! They just play and swim around."

"Tell that to the people they've maimed. Just stay in the boat until it swims away, and it won't bother you."

Jack eyed his fillets on the bank uneasily. The otter seemed to follow his gaze, and with an "Ummph!" it disappeared for an instant—only to reappear at the water's edge. It gamboled up the muddy slope, snorting happily and shaking out its fur.

"My fish!" Jack rose to jump out of the boat to protect his catch, but Marisa tapped him with warning fingers on his shoulder.

"No. Let it have them."

Trusting her woodcraft, he forced himself to inaction and stood there watching. The otter ripped apart his nice fillets with its clacking fangs, which were as big as a Doberman's but looked much sharper. When it had finished their dinner, it casually lumbered to the bank, then flipped and slid into the water on its back.

"I don't like otters anymore," said Jack, depressed.

Marisa smiled and for a split second the pain for all she had suffered left her face, but it quickly returned. Jack set her back down on a thwart and hugged her, then he put out a line and caught more fish.

They risked a cooking fire because at that time, at the end of the dry season, the Pantanal was ablaze with brush fires. A little bit of extra smoke wouldn't make much difference. Besides, the thought of eating raw fish made them ill. It wasn't dressed-up fancy and chilled like sushi—it was just plain raw. But roasted it was good, and they felt better with something in them to act as fuel.

"Where are we going now, Marisa?"

"We're on the Rio Cuiabá. In about another night and a half on the river, we should come to the Rio Paraguay, which can take us to Bolivia or even Paraguay."

"How far are we from Bolivia?"

"Close, maybe three days, but that part of Bolivia is just Pantanal like this, and I wouldn't want to leave the river and start walking in there now. It's too close to the rainy season. If we get caught out on the land when the rains come, we could find ourselves swimming, and now's not the time. Once the rivers flood their banks, all of the piranhas and the caimans will swim out on the planes in search of food. It's the most dangerous time of the year to be in the water. Once everything is flooded and the fish have spread out, it's fine, but now they're hungry. That's why I never swim in the river in the dry season unless I have to. Too many hungry fish. It's just not worth the risk."

"Do you think it will rain soon?"

"Well, we already had the first rain, remember? I can feel water in the air, and there are winds at night. It won't be long now."

"What do you think we should do, then?"

"We can do two things, I guess. We can hide in a little creek like this one somewhere and wait for the rains, so we can paddle off the river and cross into Bolivia anywhere, or we can follow the river until we get to a town. The problem with paddling into Bolivia is that there just isn't anything there, and on the other side of the wetlands is the Chaco. It's like a big desert, not a desert really, more like a big plain that goes on for hundreds of kilometers. I doubt that we could get through it.

"And anyway, we might be months waiting for it to rain enough to flood the rivers. No, I think the best idea is to get to a Bolivian town so we can catch a road that will lead us into Bolivia. There are two towns I know of that are close to the river, but I've never been to either of them, and I don't know what we are going to do once we get there. I don't even speak Spanish! I've never been out of Mato Grosso. *Papai* only bought us passports because he was going to take us to Paris."

Her voice broke, and she began to cry.

"What are we going to do, Jack? What are we going to do?"

He leaned over and hugged her. "I'll take care of that, Marisa. Don't worry. Once we get out of Brazil, I'll fix everything. I have friends in Columbia who will help us. It's not a problem. You just get us to the border, okay?"

She nodded. He hugged her tighter, but she pulled away and looked at him strangely.

"Sorry, Marisa," he said. "I understand. I won't let anyone else hurt you as long as I'm alive."

"He did hurt me, Jack, and he killed my family."

She shuddered with her misery.

Jack hurt and wished that he could help her. She'd need time. A long time. And he hoped he'd be able to see that she got it. Poor girl. Her whole world was shattered.

He looked away and noticed that night had come. Putting her back together would have to wait. Now they had to move.

"We'd better get back on the river."

They paddled out to the main channel, then motored until morning. The next night's travel brought them to the Rio Paraguay.

Jack peered ahead over the widening water, but even with the light of a bright half-moon, he couldn't see the far bank. He turned to Marisa and shouted over the outboard, "I think we've come to a lake."

"That's not a lake. It's the Paraguay. It's wide here."

She had risked running mid-river to take advantage of the stronger current, but then slowed the engine and headed toward the bank. With the Paraguay in sight, it was time for a decision.

Jack watched the bank for good place to land and for any possible danger. With arm motions, he guided her to a low spot next to a tree with a strange swollen limb that overhung the river a few feet away. He turned around to ask her why she stopped, but she pointed to the limb behind him. The swollen spot on the branch was unwinding and dropping to the river. Jack nearly fell backward when he saw it.

"Anaconda," she explained. "This is a game trail, where animals come for water." She pointed to the track beaten in the bank that led back to the brush. "He was probably waiting for his dinner."

Jack watched the seemingly endless stream of snake finally roll itself off the tree and slowly swim away.

"Don't worry, Jack. That one's too small to eat us. The big ones, though, you need to stay away from."

He didn't respond, busy thanking God they hadn't parked directly under the branch. Then he looked at her and asked, "What now?"

"Well, we have to decide where we want to go."

"How about Hollywood?" he said with a shiver. "The big snakes there are made of rubber...What are our options?"

"Well, we can go upriver to San Matias. I've never been there, but I know it's on the Rio Corixai, a tributary just upstream. Or we can go downriver to Puerto Suarez."

"Which one do you think is better?"

"I don't know. San Matias is a smaller town, and it's not a major border crossing like Puerto Suarez. The problem with San Matias is that it must be at least five days upriver, and I don't know if we have gas to get there. It's also not very far from Fonseca's ranch, so he might have people watching for us there."

"What about Puerto Suarez?"

"We can make it there in about three days, and if we run out of gas we can let the current carry us. But it's the biggest border crossing in the region, and the police will be looking for us there. It's the most obvious place to go."

"Do you think we have enough gas to carry us upriver to San Matias? We're already down to two tanks."

"You're right. We probably wouldn't make it."

"Then I guess Puerto Suarez is our only option, isn't it?"

"Yeah, I guess so."

"We'll just have to abandon the boat and hide it somewhere above town, then try to steal a car or something. We'll work something out when we get there."

"I hope so."

He smiled and said, "Where's your faith?"

His smile died when he looked into her eyes and saw that she didn't have any. For all the good she'd done in their escape—driving the truck, getting them this far through the maze of rivers, she was still in profound shock. She was lost. He'd get her back if he could, but meanwhile he had to get her out of Brazil.

"Well, we'd better get going. We still have three hours of darkness."

Chapter Twelve

"Jack, look at what I found. Bananas!" declared Marisa proudly as she held the large bunch out before her.

"That's great. I'm starving, but it's starting to look like we're going to have a real feast. I managed to catch something other than a pacu or a piranha. See that over there?" he pointed to the boat. Lying on one its thwarts was a large blue-speckled catfish with barbels twitching in the air as if it was conducting an orchestra.

"*Jóia!* Pintado. I love pintado." She grinned.

It warmed him to see it. A glimpse of the girl who led him through the trails came shining for a moment through the blackness. He smiled back at her and said, "We're going to have a great breakfast." Then he busied himself with the fire.

The trip down the Paraguay had been uneventful. They stayed close to the bank on the Bolivian side and had little trouble. They had been woken twice during their first day's sleep by the noise of outboards and a low-flying plane, but the sounds were distant and died away quickly. Then last night, they saw lights on the river behind them, but they never got close enough to worry about.

Now they were less than a night away from Puerto Suarez. They would be able to ditch their boat and walk into town well before dawn. If it was as easy as their trip downriver had been, they had nothing to worry about. He felt light and confident, and that morning, he thought he could see traces of the old Marisa.

When the fire was blazing, he filleted the fish and watched Marisa wash up with river water, cupping it and then pouring it over her face. He loved her. He knew it then, as he knew it even before they reached the mine, and now she needed him. He wanted to do anything in the world to make her happy and hoped that he could somehow fit in her equation—not as an uncle or a brother—but as a man that she could love, too. He knew that the time in which she could think of anything like that was very far away, thanks to damage wrought on her by Fonseca.

Well, it didn't matter. He'd do what he could to help her and to make her happy, and then one day, when she was healed and had put it all behind her, then maybe they could have something. He could wait, and he could even accept it if she never wanted him as he wanted her. That didn't matter. It was enough to love her and to see her happy again, and the way things were going, he might just see that.

They were almost at Puerto Suarez, and once there, he was sure he could get them to Houston. He knew how to operate in South America. All it would take would be a few phone calls to some friends and a few of their emeralds given as *propinas*. He could almost hear the engines of the plane that would take them to freedom.

Wait a minute. He shook himself from his revelry. It was a real plane he was hearing.

He stamped out the fire, called to Marisa to get beneath a tree and then scrambled into the brush himself. He strained to see the sky through the thicket, but couldn't focus on anything. He was worried. This was the worst of all the spots in which they camped. They were behind a bend in a small creek and out of view from the river, but their boat was fully exposed to the sky. There was nothing to be done. It was the best spot they could find before daylight.

He prayed that they wouldn't be spotted, and it seemed as if his prayer was answered—the engine noise slowly faded away and didn't return. They were safe. With a sigh of relief, he crawled out from under the brush, knelt down and rekindled the fire. They were eating within the hour.

"How much more river do we have until we reach Puerto Suarez, Marisa?" asked Jack as he peeled a banana.

"I'm not sure. I've only been this way twice—my father and brothers used to fish the Paraguay, but mostly farther north. I think we should make it within a few hours. Once we see the bridge, we shouldn't be too far away, but then we should be careful. If the police plan to catch us on the river, that will be where they will wait. They have a few patrol boats on the Brazilian side in Corumbá. I still can't believe that the police are chasing us, Jack. I've known the policemen in Poconé all my life. It was some of them that went off that bridge on the *Transpantaneira*."

She became sad.

"You can't think about it, Marisa. By getting rid of them you saved our lives, and we are innocent. We just have to think about getting out of here."

"I don't know what to do or how to act anywhere else, Jack. I'm Brazilian."

"Don't worry. You'll do just fine in America, and anyway, with the information we have on these computer tapes, you'll be able to return to Brazil a hero. With the money you have in emeralds, you'll be able to live in Rio in style. Your parents would have wanted that."

"Yes, they would have." She smiled sadly. "You still have to show me Rio…if you want to, I mean. You promised. Remember?"

"Of course, I remember, and I will as soon as we get out of here and get this all straightened out. Don't worry, Marisa, I'd like more than anything to see you on the beach in a bikini."

As soon as he said it, he saw the pain in her eyes.

"I'm sorry, that was a stupid thing to say."

"It's all right, Jack. I wasn't a virgin, or anything. I'm from a small town, but I'm not a small-town girl. What that man did to me, though, hurt me, Jack. It's going to take me a long time to get back together again, and that's just the small part of it. They murdered my parents! I'm all alone."

He could see her start to fall apart as she had every morning when she finished her night's work of piloting the river.

"Don't think of it, Marisa. Not now. Let's just think of getting out of here. Freedom and justice are close, just a day away. Keep yourself together until we make it. And remember, I'm here and will be here as long as you want me to be. I'm responsible for much of your trouble, and I'll do all I can to set things straight."

He wanted to say that he'd like to kill the mother fuckers, but didn't see the point. They just had to keep their heads clear and survive. The rest would come later.

"You going to be okay?"

She forced a brave smile, which was false, but which was a good sign for both of them. If she could endure, he knew that she could make it. Even if she just wanted to put him at ease, that meant that she was trying.

"That's a girl. Now let's get some sleep. We have a long night ahead of us."

They climbed back in the boat and curled up. Soon they were both fast asleep.

*   *   *   *

The sharp crack of pistol shots cut the air and ripped into the wooden planks of their boat. Jack woke up and scrambled to his feet to find himself face-to-face with José, who was standing in the bow of a motorboat not more than ten feet away.

"It's them," José said to the man behind him who was drawing a small, silent trawling motor up out of the muddy water. "We've been looking for you for a long time. You might have made it if one of our planes hadn't spotted your smoke and your boat this morning."

Jack cursed himself for his carelessness.

"Oh, don't be so hard on yourself. You impress me, *gringo*. I didn't think you would make it nearly this far."

The other man in the boat walked past José, jumped to the bank and pulled their bow up and out of the water. Once they were secure, José hopped down, still keeping his gun on Jack. Marisa, who woke up with the gunshots, peered over the gunnel, terrified.

"You know, because you've managed to do so well for yourself, and since you gave me the opportunity to shoot that grating little rat, Hernanie, I almost want to let you go. It would be fun to watch the senator sweat. But I can't do that. You know too much. And even if you didn't, I still couldn't let you go, not without paying back the favor that you did to my face."

José struck Jack hard in the nose with his pistol, knocking him clear of his boat and heavily to the ground.

"Get up."

Jack tried to stagger to his feet while clutching his shattered nose, but José didn't give him the chance. Silver shone in the air as his boot connected with Jack's chin, flipping him backward and back to earth. José smiled and stretched out his arm to aim down at the dazed man bleeding in the dust. "Goodbye, *gringo*. It's been fun."

"NO!"

He turned to see Marisa standing in the boat, clasping her hands to her cheeks in horror. José looked her over. The five days since their escape had done much to heal her bruises, and she was beautiful again.

"No?" he asked.

"No! Please. Please, don't kill him."

He looked at her, pensive, then his eyes narrowed.

"Okay. I won't, not yet. I think I'd like him to see this." He looked to the boat driver. "Get him up."

The man pulled Jack up and helped him gain his balance.

"Keep an eye on him and shoot him if he moves."

He handed the gun to the other man, then he moved toward Marisa, pulling off his shirt and unbuckling his belt as he walked closer.

"No," she murmured. "No. Don't. Please. Please." She hugged herself and kneeled down below the thwarts. "Please..."

He grabbed her by the hair and dragged her out of the boat onto to the dusty shore. Her sobs sounded as he ripped off her shirt and struggled her jeans down off her brown thighs. He kicked apart her legs and fondled her roughly while she whimpered, crossed her arms over her naked breasts and pleaded for him to stop. Jack looked on, raging but inert, covered by the man with the pistol.

José ripped away her panties, leaving a nasty welt where they parted, and then he pulled down his pants. Marisa stared to the sky as if in prayer for a quick release from the chains of flesh that held her to the earth, and didn't even flinch when he entered her.

She didn't feel it. She wasn't there. She was in a special place where neither he nor the senator could touch her, in a place they could never reach. She was in the darkness with her memories, with her parents and her brothers, and maybe soon with Jack who would come to be there with her. Pain was the legacy left to them by the spirit of their dream.

They had found their mine, but what had it brought them? What was the price yet left to pay? She thought of the green crystals they had pulled from the earth and of that special one that her father had presented her mother to celebrate their victory and to welcome their new life. She thought of her mother's necklace and almost thought she saw it, somewhere high above her, flashing in the light. It was there!

She focused and saw it swinging above her eyes, her mother's emerald chained to the sweaty neck that strained and pulled above her. She came alive, pulsing with hate and vengeance for her own violation and for her mother's death. Lunging up, she bit him hard on the shoulder, where its muscles met the neck, with all the force she had.

"AAGGHH!" screamed José.

Jack's guard swiveled with the noise, which was fatal. For as soon as he looked away, Jack grabbed the barrel of his pistol, held it wide and then delivered several sharp, open-handed blows beneath his lower jaw. The man was momentarily stunned, so Jack took advantage and brought him to earth with a bone-breaking kick to the knee, which caused him to drop the pistol. Jack picked it up and shot him twice in the chest. Then he raced over to pull José off of Marisa.

Jack would have shot the Colombian in the back, as he crouched there between her legs, pummeling her mercilessly in the face, but he was afraid that the bullet would pass through and hit her, too, so Jack grabbed him by the hair and wrenched him clear of her for a shot. The Colombian was quick and got a hand on the gun as Jack brought it down to fire. The shot went wide as they fell to the ground together in a rolling grapple, each trying to control the pistol.

The Colombian struck Jack in his crushed nose, causing him to spin away in pain. Then he drew himself up to press his advantage and strike again, but as he did so, he pushed his thigh into the gun. Jack fired, and they both recoiled in pain.

The bullet grazed José's leg, causing him no real damage except to bleed profusely. The real loser was Jack. He didn't have a proper grip when he pulled the trigger, and the automatic's slide wrenched his thumb back savagely.

The pistol lay between them. Both struggled toward it, and Jack was first. His injured hand failed him when he tried to pick it up. The Colombian kicked the gun free, then dove after it. He scrambled to his feet to stand before Jack, triumphant, and drew a slow bead to fire.

"AAGGHH!!" The Columbian's shot went wild as he doubled up, breathless. Marisa stood behind him with a heavy branch, which she swung back like a pinch hitter to strike him again. She knocked him into the water like a grounder shot past first base.

On seeing a chance, Jack stumbled up and rushed to dive in after him.

"No!" Marisa commanded.

He stopped at the water's edge, just as José popped to the surface about 10 feet out with the pistol still in hand, already aimed to shore. He smiled evilly at Jack, but his smile faded quickly with the sight of boiling water around him. A school of ravenous piranha had caught the scent of his bloodied leg, and now he was their feast. With a shriek he lunged toward shore, but his flayed legs failed him. José splashed headlong and disappeared. The water reddened with his blood.

Jack held Marisa to him and helped her cry it out.

In her hand, she held her mother's necklace.

Chapter Thirteen

It had been a long day during which neither Jack nor Marisa could sleep, but it had finally ended, and they were both in better spirits. With the nightmare of José and his henchman behind them, they were moving down the river, ready to escape Brazil, for the moment, anyway.

They had made a pact that afternoon to put an end to Fonseca and his evil after their own lives were secured. For them both, it meant everything. What the senator had done to Marisa's family, they swore would never happen to her country. Once away in America, safe with the information they had, they could help the U.S. government to dispose of him. That was their plan. The fortune of emeralds that tinkled around the computer back-up tape in the satchel seemed secondary. They had a mission. They were going to bury Fonseca, as he had buried her parents.

Although just raped for the second time in her life and for the second time in a week, Marisa exhibited more of herself that evening than Jack had seen since they escaped the Fonseca ranch.

She had saved his life once again by keeping him out of the water, and by watching the death of one of her rapists and her mother's killer, she had begun to walk the long road back to finding her own inner peace. But there was more than that. Through all that happened, a bond had been forged between them that would be there when all the crying was done, when they could both smile again. Jack wasn't sure what it was and knew he wouldn't know anytime soon, but for good or for bad, they were linked together through experience, through debt and through affection. They would do anything for one another. They were family, though exactly what their roles were, he couldn't say. He wanted her for himself alone, but he wanted her any way she came. Mostly, though, he wanted her alive, and he prayed that their trip down river and their escape through Bolivia would provide that.

They had been on the river for little more than three hours and already the lights on the bridge that linked Corumbá to Puerto Suarez loomed in the distance, maybe ten miles downriver. They had traded their old, wooden longboat for José's fiberglass cruiser with its twin 90-horse outboards and had roared down the river, hugging close to the Bolivian shoreline. It wouldn't be long before they left the river. They just needed to make the outskirts of the city, which they were quickly nearing.

Marisa guided them even closer to the bank and cut back the engines. They needed to be as quiet as possible. As they neared the bridge, they could see patrol boats sweeping searchlights beneath it. They were still hunted, so they needed to be careful.

As they idled in yet closer, they could make out a long line of headlights on the Brazilian side at the approach to the bridge. It must have been a roadblock ordered to search for them in the hundreds of trucks that rumbled commerce back and forth across the border. It was good that they came by boat.

When they motored as far as they felt safe, Marisa nosed into the bank and they disembarked. Jack had spent three hours shoveling earth into the boat before they left camp and had pulled the rubber ball from their boat plug. He pulled the plug then, and the boat began to take on water.

Loaded as it was with earth and its heavy engines, the boat sank within minutes. When the bow passed under, they climbed up the bank and began the long walk into town, carrying nothing more than the clothes they wore on their backs, two water bottles, The Professor's leather pouch that contained their emeralds and the computer tapes detailing Fonseca's drug smuggling ring.

It was almost 11 p.m. when they walked into town, and as good luck would have it, the streets were deserted. It was Monday night. Staying in the shadows, they hurried down side streets and headed west until they were several kilometers from the river, then they moved south until they came to the two-lane highway that connected the frontier lowlands to the highland town of Santa Cruz and eventually to the capital of La Paz. Once in La Paz, Jack knew that he could buy them freedom. They were on their way, but how to get there?

As they crouched in the trees, they watched a dozen trucks roll by full of the commerce that the free-market reforms had opened between the countries over the last few years, but very few private cars drove past. Cars were for commuting in South America, and people who owned them were reluctant to use them on the pot-holed ruts that passed as highways between towns. Hitchhiking wasn't an option, and it wouldn't do to rent a car, either. All they had to barter with was emerald rough. And to steal a car? That would make them outlaws in yet another country. No, the best way to make it to La Paz was to sneak a ride on a truck, preferably without the driver's knowledge.

"Come on, Marisa."

"Where are we going to go?"

"To a truck stop. We're going to get a ride."

He led her down the path that paralleled the tiny but busy highway, until they came to a gas station/restaurant a mile past the outskirts of town. Its parking lot was full of loaded, flatbed trucks. They sat on the edge of the parking lot, out of the light, trying to figure out which one would be their best bet. After pondering awhile, Jack slunk into the lot and had a look around. Fifteen minutes of looking led him to a decision: an empty flatbed with Bolivian plates and a tarpaulin stretched out to conceal its empty hold. He figured it was probably headed home after having delivered a load. He waved Marisa out of the dark and over to him.

When he explained his reasoning to her, she asked, "Well, how do we know that it isn't going to Brazil to pick something up?"

"We don't, but I've thought of that. We'll just have to keep an eye out once we leave the lot to see which way we're headed. If we start back toward town, we'll have to jump out and try another one."

She agreed it was the best thing they could do, so they both climbed in and waited. They waited for over an hour with still no sound or sign of the driver. While they waited, exhaustion overwhelmed them both and cast them deep into sleep before the driver finally finished his last beer, and returned to gear up and weave out onto the highway.

Chapter Fourteen

Marisa woke to the smell of diesel and incessant bumping. She was hot with the sunlight that beamed down upon the tarpaulin above her and that had turned the flatbed into a furnace. At first she wondered where she was and wondered where her parents were. A pothole shook the truck and brought back her memory with a spine-numbing jolt. They were in a truck, and it was daylight. She nudged the man beside her whose swollen nose and lips made him look more duck than human. *Poor dear man*, she thought as she shook him.

"Jack. Jack. We're moving!"

He struggled up to consciousness and murmured, "Go back to sleep; it's just a dream."

"No, it's not a dream. We're moving. The truck left the parking lot, and it's daytime."

His eyelids fluttered like slow-speed shutters on a camera.

"What?"

He rubbed his eyes and sat up. His back hurt from sleeping on the metal bed.

"We're moving, Jack."

"Where are we going?"

"I don't know. We were supposed to find that out before we went to sleep, remember."

He looked at her dumbly, then slowly regained the situation. "Right," he agreed. "We overslept?"

"Yes. We did."

Jack crawled to the back of the truck then peered out under the tarpaulin. It was the same, flat terrain that he had driven through on his way from Cuiabá to Poconé. But that didn't tell him anything.

"Where are we?"

He didn't answer. He was looking for clues. A passing billboard gave him all he needed: *Sempre Vida. Sempre Coca-Cola.* It was in Portuguese, not in Spanish. They were back in Brazil, heading away from the border.

"You don't want to know."

"You mean we're back in Brazil?"

He nodded.

"What are we going to do?" she asked in despair.

"I don't know, but I have a friend in Rio. If we can get there, he will help us out. I'm sure of it."

She reached out to him and held him tight, then looked at his battered face. It was worse than hers after José had hit her. They were a pair, bookends carved by the evil of man. She touched his nose, and he flinched.

"Ouch…I'm not much to look at, am I?"

"I'm sure you look better than me," she said rubbing her lip. "I must be awful."

"You're beautiful, more beautiful than I've ever seen you, and you saved my life again." He leaned down to gently kiss both her blackened eyes.

She smiled, though it hurt, then drew herself away.

"I didn't save your life. You saved mine, and you gave me myself back, part of me, anyway. You were so brave, Jack. Nobody has ever been so good to me. Back there on the river, pulling that man away from me, and back at the ranch—you didn't have to come back for me. If you hadn't, you would probably already be out of trouble."

He laughed and said, "If I hadn't gone back for my guide, I'd probably be in the belly of a snake or a giant river otter, and besides, it's not often that I get the chance to monopolize the attention of a girl like you. No, everything I've done has been for purely selfish motives. I want exclusivity in selling your emeralds for you, too, remember?"

"You have it, Jack. You know that."

He wished he had more. After all that had happened to her in the last week, he knew it might be a lifetime's wait for her to be ready for what he most wanted, and besides, he was still too old for her. Three weeks in the swamp and several beatings hadn't made him any younger.

They lay down on the bed of the truck, and as tired as they were, they fell back asleep. The bright, yellow sunlight had intensified when they were again awoken, this time by a combination of the stifling heat and by the sounds of downshifting to slow the truck.

Jack looked at his watch—10:30 a.m.—then he crawled to the tailgate to peer out. They had passed through a gate and were rolling to a halt somewhere in the shade of a large aluminum cowling. Jack heard the driver climb out of the cab and crunch away across the macadam. He took a chance and stuck his head out. They were the last in a line of trucks waiting to be filled by a giant hopper. Grain dust filled the air.

He moved to the front of the bed and struggled through the tarpaulin to look through the cab and front windshield. Men were uncovering the bed of the truck in front of them. They had to risk it. He grabbed Marisa's hand. "Come on!"

They scrambled out over the large tailgate and ran to a shadowed corner, behind a pile of sacks. They were just in time. A crew walked up from behind a silo and began unlacing their tarpaulin. Once the vinyl was clear of the bed, a member of the crew hopped into the cab and eased their truck forward. With a signal from the foreman, their hiding place of the previous night disappeared under a rain of soybeans with a *whoosh*.

A line had formed behind their truck, which prevented them from leaving their shelter to re-enter it. It rolled out from the head of the line and then turned out of the gate, probably back to Bolivia, Jack thought sadly. It was a forlorn moment, but short lasting. It was soon replaced by fear—fear of the khaki-colored rumps of two well-fed policemen who took seats on the sacks above them. They were drinking coffee and talking with the co-op manager.

"So, have you had any more trouble with bums coming through the fence to steal soybean meal?"

"Not since you took care of the last two—which doesn't surprise me. I don't imagine anyone else would dare to try."

The policeman smiled. "It was the least we could do for you, *amigo*. You are a generous man, so naturally we send out special signals to the criminal element on your behalf. This *café* is excellent by the way."

"I'm glad you like it. Now tell me what's going on with that crazy American. Is it true that he murdered Hernanie Fonseca?"

"It seems so. That little rat Hernanie won't be knocking the girls around in the whorehouses out here anymore. The American shot him in the gut and let him bleed to death, which was fitting, but what he did to that poor woman was without excuse!"

"Why, what did he do?"

"The American suffocated her with a live parrot. I heard it was a very ugly scene. And now the bastard has her daughter!"

Marisa started, but Jack warned her from sound with a squeeze to her elbow.

"Do you think that he will harm her?"

"I'm afraid so. Apparently, he is some sort of mass murderer who fled down here to escape his own police. It is said that he killed several people when he stole an airplane to make his escape. Orders from above say that he is extremely dangerous, and we aren't to take any chances. We are to shoot him without regard for the girl. In fact, she might now be dangerous also. He seems to have some sort of hypnotic power and can turn other people into killers like himself. Apparently, he has done this several times before in the U.S. and in Mexico. Our captain told us to be very careful if we spot either of them, and to treat the girl as if she is as dangerous as he.

"It's a sad thing, because she is supposed to be very beautiful, sort of a legend around Poconé, but you can be sure that, pretty or not, my life is more important than hers." He patted his holster. "Right, Germano?"

His partner nodded, "*Puxa*! I'd shoot her in a second. This stuff scares the piss out of me. It's not just normal crime—it's *macumba* or some other kind of witchcraft we're dealing with, if you ask me. It sounds like the man could be a demon, or at least, possessed by one. Maybe she's a demon now, too. What kind of person would kill with a parrot. It's sick. He's evil and cruel."

The manager finished his cup and asked, "Do you think he'll get away?"

"I don't see how he could. There are helicopters in the air and boats in the water. We also have roadblocks on every road leaving the state and are searching everyone who passes through. Everyone. That's why we're here. We're supposed to check every truck you load and stamp their manifests when we're done. That should speed things at the roadblocks. As it is now, traffic's lined up for kilometers, and it's even worse at Puerto Suarez. Bolivian customs is unloading every truck. They think this fellow is Satan incarnate."

"You have to inspect all our loads? You can't be serious. Why, that will take hours!"

The police corporal smiled and then stood. "Yes, we have orders from Senator Fonseca himself, but we don't have to inspect them that closely, do we? He just wants us make sure that the American murderer doesn't try to sneak out in a soybean sack, but what would that bastard be doing in a granary? No, it's just a formality and will go quickly. Why don't you just have the manifests brought up to your office. It's a much more comfortable place to work, and besides, didn't you say that you had a little something for us?"

"Of course. Sure. Is it already that time of the month again? How could I have forgotten? Come on, let's get out of the heat. I'm sure your inspections will be more efficient in the air-conditioning."

When the khaki rumps above them disappeared, Marisa whispered to Jack, "What are we going to do? They'll shoot us on sight."

"Then we'd better not be seen. We'd better try get on a truck headed back to Rio where my friend can help us. If I can get these computer files to the States, we'll be protected. My country is very anti-drug. Let's get on one of those trucks and get out of here."

They sat and watched for over an hour, but there were too many people for them to make their move. The sounding of the lunch whistle brought a chance, though, when all the workers abandoned the area for the *futebol* field.

Seeing no one in sight, they sprinted for a line of parked trucks only ten or twenty yards away, which they darted behind to get out of sight. Jack moved from one to another until he found the RJ license plate denoting Rio de Janeiro. He signaled to Marisa to follow, then they both climbed up under the tarpaulin and aboard. It was full of bagged soybean flour. They dug through the sacks and tunneled themselves into a cave invisible from above, in case the lazy policemen decided to have a quick look at the cargo in an extraordinary display of duty.

They lay there quietly, listening to the slight sounds of *futebol* playing out across the yard, until it was slowly replaced by the sounds of industry after the whistle blew to end the two-hour lunch break. Before long, their truck was idling. Then it popped into gear, and they were slowly on their way, hopefully toward Rio.

Chapter Fifteen

J ack bulled the sacks off them once their truck ground up to speed after an interminable wait at the roadblock. They had agonized for hours, hoping beyond hope that they wouldn't be discovered by searching police, and they had sweat, crushed down under the heavy sacks that roasted with the afternoon heat, magnified and trapped in by the tarpaulin above them.

"God, I'm thirsty," he said, as he pushed and piled and rearranged the sacks into a crude bunker around them. "Are you sure there isn't any water left, Marisa?"

"No. You know we just finished the last of it."

He knew, and it hadn't helped a bit to slake their thirst. He cursed himself for not taking more water when they left the river. Marisa had filled all three of the plastic bottles they'd found on José's boat, but Jack told her to leave one behind. He didn't want to hassle with the weight, but now, muddy or not, that last bottle would have tasted like Dom Perignon. Well, it didn't do any good to think about it. They had other problems—hunger for one—to deal with.

"Can you eat soybean flour?"

"Well, that's what it is made for, though I've never eaten it raw before," she responded as she squirmed on the hard sacks, trying to find a comfortable seat.

"Well, then let's have lunch." Jack tore open one of the sacks with the dull blade of his pocketknife, and the whitish tan powder spilled out over his damp shirt, breading him like a chicken.

"Shit," he muttered as he tried to stem the flow.

The bag stopped pouring when a hard, plastic corner of a package poked out to seal it.

"What's that?" asked Marisa, as Jack worked it out of the bag.

He held it in his hands, a four-pound brick of a different powder, wrapped tightly in plastic.

"It's cocaine."

They had managed to hitch a ride with one of the drug shipments. No wonder the police had been dispatched to clear the trucks before they left the co-op. Fonseca was protecting his drugs from his own roadblocks.

Marisa looked at the sack, then looked away upon seeing the label.

"I guess this is good for us, anyway," said Jack. "Since this truck's carrying the senator's dope, it will be sure to get through to its destination on time. Here, try some of this."

He poured some of the flour into her hands then tried a handful himself. It set up in his mouth like quick-drying cement, soaking up his saliva in seconds. "Yuck," he sputtered, while spitting it out. "This is awful." He worked his tongue in and out to dislodge the paste that caked his gums, then he wiped the sweat that dripped from his forehead with the hands that held the flour.

Marisa, though thirsty and hungry, chuckled when he did.

"What's so funny?" he asked, working his tongue around.

"You are. You look like Casper!" He ran a finger across his cheek, and it came back white. He laughed, too. It was good to see her smile.

With nothing else to do, they laid down to rest a while longer. Jack wanted to hold her, but sensitive to what had recently happened, he tried to keep his distance to ease her. But she wanted him near, so she curled her head onto his chest and soon fell fast asleep. He watched her as they moved on, he watched and prayed for help and for a drink of water.

*   *   *   *

It was dark when Jack awoke to a drumming sound—rain ricocheting hard off the tarp, which was swollen in the middle with a growing puddle.

"Marisa, wake up and get the water bottle!" She awoke quickly and felt around the bottom of the truck until she found it wedged between some sacks. Once she freed the bottle, he grabbed it and stood below the tarp, heavy with water. A slit from his pocketknife brought a cascade down upon them and into the bottle, which filled quickly. Jack passed it down to Marisa who nearly downed the entire two liters, while he stood above her like a calf at an udder drinking until he could hold no more. Then they bathed themselves, reveling in the coolness of the flood.

"I love rain," said Marisa as she held her face up to the captive torrent and ran it through her hair. He loved her as he watched her. She smiled and seemed almost happy then.

Her smile withered when the truck stopped. "What is it?" she whispered. "Do you think he heard us?"

"I don't think so." Jack looked at his watch. It's luminous dial read 8:30 p.m. "The driver is probably taking a dinner break. Or maybe he's stopping for gas or to sleep. He can't drive forever."

"I'm scared."

"It'll be all right." Jack climbed up the tiered sacks and peered out from under the tarp. He had guessed correctly. They were at one of the many truck stops that dotted the country, outposts of civilization in an otherwise empty land, like oases on the old silk road.

Their driver, apparently not wanting to chance getting boxed in by another rig, had parked well away from the gas pumps and the restaurant, leaving the truck in darkness. Wanting a better look, Jack worked his head and shoulders out from under the tarp. The lot was empty, and the pumps were manned by a solitary attendant who leaned back on a diesel pump, apparently asleep. The only movement came from inside the restaurant, where several truckers were belly to the bar drinking beer, eating meat and beans, and listening to the teary strains of *Música Sertaneija*, Brazilian country and western. On an outside corner of the building, next to the public toilets, was a pay phone. He decided to risk being seen to make a call.

"I'll be right back, Marisa."

"Where are you going?"

"To call for help."

"Be careful!" she whispered.

He nodded, climbed out and down to the muddy parking lot, then moved slowly to the phone. Flicking quickly through his wallet, that he had miraculously managed to keep, he found Itzhak's number and dialed collect. After several tries, the call went through.

"Hello Itzhak, this is Jack..."

"Jackson! Jackson Brown, how good of you to call. We've been expecting your call."

"We?"

"Yes, we! Myself and all of your other friends. They have been by quite often lately. I think that they want to throw a surprise party for you when you get here."

Jack swallowed. "Really?"

"Oh yes. You have made some very important friends here, and they would like to see you."

He closed his eyes. "Do you know why?"

"Only that you have made quite an impression with them, but their explanation seems hard for me to believe."

"Don't believe it, Itzhak. I have certain valuable information, something they want badly. What do you suggest."

"I don't know what to suggest, Mr. Brown. But if I were you, I might talk to your government people before I made a deal. They carry a lot of weight. Talk to them before you make any decisions. Rio is hot this time of year, very hot, jumping more than it does during *Carnaval*, and sadly, it's not a safe place for you Canadians. I think we've talked long enough. Talk to your officials. Maybe they can help you work out the best possible business arrangements. Goodbye."

The line went dead. Jack hung up and turned around to face a big, dark man behind him.

"*Qual é, Meu Irmão*? What's going on, brother? Calling home or the lady friend down the road?" It was just a truck driver.

He smiled, though he didn't want to, and replied, "Would I waste a nickel on the wife?"

"That's true, but listen—you'd better grab a shower first, *amigo*. Smells like too many hours at the wheel."

Jack patted the man on the shoulder then walked nonchalantly through the rain back to his truck.

"Well?" asked Marisa as he climbed back into the bed.

"Not good," he confessed. "My friend says the police have been asking about us and are watching for us there.

He thinks that maybe we should try to get to my embassy in Brasília."

"Brasília? I have an uncle in Brasília, my mother's younger brother, my only living relative. He's a major in the Army."

"Would he help us?"

"Family always helps in Brazil. *Futebol*, family, friends, then flag, always in that order."

"Well, I guess we'd better try him. I'm out of friends in this country who could help. Now we have to figure out how to get to Brasília."

"We're on our way there now, if this truck is really bound for Rio. There is only one decent road from this part of Brazil to Rio, and it goes through the capital to get there. This is it."

"Good. Well, I guess we'd better get some sleep."

"Okay, but first we eat."

"No thanks, Marisa. I don't think I can handle anymore soybean flour."

"You don't have to. Here." She pulled an orange from a sack and handed it to him. "I stole them off another truck."

Chapter Sixteen

With the green of the traffic light, the truck rumbled on, leaving Jack and Marisa to watch it disappear into the gloom beyond the streetlamps. It was 2 a.m., pouring rain, without a soul in sight, but who would be? They were on the outskirts of Brasília, standing in front of a large, gated entrance painted bright with the silhouettes of a toucan and a lion. They were at the zoo.

Marisa spied some public phones besides the unmanned gate and wasted no time in splashing over to them.

"Are you sure we can trust your uncle?" asked Jack, who shivered as the rain ran down his face, obscuring his vision and draining all his warmth.

"Of course we can. He's my uncle. I don't know what he can do for us, but at least he'll get us out of the rain. Anyway, what other options do we have?"

"None. You're right. Go ahead and call him."

Since she didn't have his number, Marisa spent the next half-hour arguing with operators and continually re-dialing until she finally got through. "It's ringing, Jack."

He moved closer.

"*Alô,*" she shouted. "Hello! *Tio* Marcello? It's me, Marisa... No, I'm fine. Yes, I'm fine. No, it's not like that at all. I'm here in Brasília... Yes, Brasília, standing in front of the zoo. I'm here with a friend... a friend! He's okay, *tio*.

No, that's not what happened. Look, I'll explain it to you when you come, and listen, *tio*, no police. They have it all wrong. They're dangerous to me... No, nothing like that. Please, just come by yourself, and I'll explain it all when you get here... *Um beijo, tio. Tchau.*" She hung up and turned to Jack, who was huddling with her in the slim protection of the telephone housing.

"He's coming. You know I haven't seen my uncle in eight years. I wonder if he'll recognize me."

"He'll figure it out one way or another. We're the only lunatics standing in the rain in front of the zoo at this hour. Come on, Marisa. I think we'd better hide behind those bushes by the fence. I'd hate to be picked up now, after all we've been through."

They pushed behind the bushes that skirted the entrance. The bushes cut the sting of the rain a bit, but more importantly, they were concealing and afforded a good view of the road and the field that separated them from it. Nobody would be able to get near them without their knowing. Jack didn't know that he could trust Marisa's uncle, and being hidden would buy them a little time if they had to get away.

An hour passed without any sign of her uncle or any break in the rain. Even in the tropics, rain can chill the skin, and they were shaking with it.

"*Jesus*, Marisa, it's been an hour. Do you think he's coming?"

"Of course he's coming. Maybe he lives far away, but I'm sure he'll be here soon."

"You don't think he called the police, do you?"

"Jack, I told him not to. Don't be silly. He's my uncle."

As soon as she had spoken, an arm gripped Jack in a stranglehold around the throat and a pistol barrel pressed hard to his temple while a voice behind him shouted, "Step back, Marisa! I've got him."

"No, Uncle. No! He's my friend! He saved my life!"

Jack would have said something in his own defense, but the arm had tensed around his neck and he couldn't even breathe. The lights were going out fast, and because of the pistol, he couldn't struggle to resist.

"*Tio*, don't kill him!" were the last words he heard before he lost consciousness.

He came to, gasping to see the concerned face of Marisa hovering above him and another face standing just beyond hers, a face painted dark, almost hidden in a black balaclava. The man pulled her back, "Let him get his bearings. They always come up fighting."

And Jack did. As soon as he was awake, he was on his feet groping for the arm around his neck that wasn't there.

"Sorry about the rough treatment," said the man behind Marisa. He pulled off his hood to reveal a handsome, rugged face similar to hers.

Jack panted to regain his breath and coughed, "It's okay. I'm starting to get used to it."

The man holstered his pistol.

"I'm Marisa's uncle, Marcello."

Jack rubbed his neck and said, "You have a hell of a way with introductions."

"Sorry about that. I would have killed you if Marisa hadn't shouted for me not to. You're a famous man these days. A double murderer."

"I didn't kill your sister."

"Marisa told me, but let's not talk here. It's not safe. Follow me."

He led them in a running crouch around the perimeter fence to his car that was parked behind some trees almost a kilometer away. Jack and Marisa worked hard to catch their breath as they began driving away.

"What the hell are you, Marcello, some kind of ninja?" asked Jack as they drove onto the main highway that led into the South side of the city.

"Ninja? No…I used to be in Army Special Forces and jungle warfare."

"Could have fooled me. You look like you came straight from Kyoto or a comic book."

"No, not Japan. I wish. I got all this gear in North Carolina, years ago when I was training with your Army. It's the first chance I ever had to use it other than in training. Nice stuff, eh?"

"I'll say. You're in special forces?"

"I used to be, but not anymore. That's for younger men."

"You seem young enough to me." Jack massaged his sore Adam's apple. "What does an older man like you do nowadays, other than sneak around the zoo at night?"

"I guard the president."

* * * *

Marcello paced back and forth in front of the others, who had showered and were dressed in warm terry robes. Jack and Marisa were both stuffed and seated behind their empty dinner plates at the kitchen table.

"So that bastard Fonseca was behind poor Isabella's death. *Filho-da-puta*, I'd like to break his fat neck with my own hands."

They had recounted the whole story to the major, except for the rapes Marisa suffered. Jack thought Marcello noticed the rents in the fabric of their story, but if he did, he let it pass. He had become more and more agitated as he listened, until he could do nothing but pace around the room and clinch his hands behind his back. He was a lean man in his late thirties or early forties, but had the taut body of a college wrestler. He bounced on the balls of his feet back and forth between the oven and the freezer, pacing faster with each passing minute.

"*Filho-da-mãe*, son of a bitch. I'd like to break every bone in his fat body. Bastard. But what are we to do? How can we best use these computer tapes?"

"Why not give them to the news media?" asked Jack.

"That might not be a good idea. Fonseca is the darling of the biggest TV network and newspaper chain—he is a large stockholder—and even if we gave them to opposition papers, we have no guarantee that the information in them would ever be published. It's too valuable and too dangerous. Somebody might sell the tapes back to him for political favors or for power, and you can bet if he gets them back, he won't allow either of you to live. It wouldn't matter where you went, either. People with the kind of connections and money he has could find you anywhere in the world."

"What about the police?"

"Forget it. You have the police chasing you all over the country already, with orders to shoot you on sight. He has them in his pocket."

"My friend in Rio suggested that we try to get the information to my government."

"Now, that might not be a bad idea! They are very, very anti-drug, and pressure applied from them weighs heavily here in Brasília. Our government usually cries foul and complains about American imperialism, but they generally do what the U.S. asks of them—anything for new loans or the chance of debt relief. But Fonseca's their golden boy. They dropped poor President Risolia like a brick when he

171

started falling in the poles. Your ambassador is always very polite and deferential to the president, but your government doesn't seem willing to deal with him on anything now. It's no secret that they have aligned themselves with Fonseca. It's ridiculous! His party controls both houses of the legislature and has defeated every bit of good legislation that *Presidente* Risolia sent to them. Now they claim to want the same things he does, and everybody seems to believe them.

Only an idiot would vote for the bastard or anybody else in his coalition if they bothered to follow their legislative voting record, but nobody does. Politics don't work that way here. Nobody reads, and even if they did, the newspapers are controlled by politicians. Elections are won with free T-shirts, free beer, dances, and lots and lots of money. They buy the votes of the poor for a song. Then they make sure the poor remain poor until the next round of elections when they can buy their votes again. *Filho de mãe*. Maybe the best thing that could happen to Brazil would be if we, the military, took over government, but we won't. Not again. The people want democracy, and we will ensure that they have it, even if it means watching our country slip into nothingness. Murdering bastard."

He paced on, then remembering himself, he turned and said, "Let me get you some more hot tea, little niece. It will warm you up. And for you, Jack, I'll bring another whiskey. Good Scotch will smoke out any chill. Are you sure you don't want anything else to eat?"

"Oh no, *tio*. I'm about to burst."

"Me too," said Jack, "but another whiskey would be great."

Marcello poured the tea and whiskey.

Jack took a sip of the Scotch and asked, "So you think that my government's the best answer."

Marcello considered the question for a long moment. Finally, he looked to Jack and responded, "Yes, maybe it is the best thing. Your government seems to function better than ours, and it has power here. I'm afraid that your evidence might get handily mislaid here even if we were to give it to the chief justice of the *Supremo Tribunal Federal* himself. And even if an investigation were called for, Fonseca could stall it for years, waiting for you two to have a tragic accident.

"No, the best bet would be to get to your embassy with your emeralds and your tapes and that brick of cocaine. They will give Marisa asylum for information like you say you have here. They have the power to bring down and destroy Fonseca. I sometimes think your president has more power here than ours does at the moment. He's a lone good man in a government full of bad ones, so it's hard for him to control it.

"Yes, let's try to get you to your embassy tomorrow. We can call them in the morning, but right now you two had better get some sleep. Marisa, you can sleep in the guest bedroom down the hall, and Jack you can sleep on the living room sofa. It may not be that comfortable, but it's better than the back of a truck, I'll bet."

"Goodnight, *Tio*," said Marisa as she gave him a hug and two kisses. "Goodnight, Jack."

"Goodnight, Marisa." Jack bent down to hug her.

Marcello noted her expression with surprise as she kissed Jack's cheek, though he didn't say anything. She looked at Jack the same way that his sister, Isabella, had looked at Joaquim Fontes thirty years before. But there was something else there too, like shellshock or fear, something powerful and bad. He liked the American who had done so much for his niece and who had avenged his sister's death. It was good that he was with her.

Jack watched Marisa walk down the hall, until Marcello brought him back to earth. "Come on, Jack, help me with these bed sheets."

Chapter Seventeen

J ack felt somewhat ridiculous decked out in the boots and riding breeches of the Brazilian cavalry, but Marcello thought it was a good precaution. The national newspapers and television were flooded with his picture, but the major thought the old uniform and the close-cropped haircut he'd given Jack that morning would combine well enough with Jack's broken nose and blackened eyes to disguise him from anyone, even his own mother. Jack looked like an unfortunate officer who was limping back to his first day of work after rolling his car over the weekend.

"So, you know what to do?" Marcello glanced at him briefly before looking back to traffic.

"You drop me off at the bus station and drive on. Then I make my phone call. If the ambassador sounds strange, or if the line sounds strange, I hang up."

"But you must hang up after four minutes, no matter what."

"I was just going to say that!"

"Sorry. What then?"

"Once I hang up, I take a taxi to the Macro supermarket down the street where you will pick me up."

"Right, I'll follow your cab, the whole time. It's better like this. This way, if something bad does happen, I'll be in a better position to get you out than I would be if I were standing by your side."

"Sounds good to me, Marcello. Don't forget to get me out of trouble. Where's your ninja suit?"

"In the wash. In daylight, it's better to look like a banker," said Marcello, and in a dark suit, that's exactly what he looked like, though leaner than most.

"Okay, Jack. Here we are, and here are some tokens for the phone and some money for the cab."

"Thanks, Marcello. I owe you."

"Pay me back later. Just remember not to talk longer than four minutes. If they've set up a wiretap, they'll be able to locate you in that amount of time, and with Fonseca behind this, they'll be set to intercept you fast."

"How do you know all of this, Marcello?"

"Because that's how we catch nuts who harass the president. Our presidents aren't world powerful like yours are, but there are still plenty of crazies out there who'd like to shoot them. I might take a crack at Fonseca myself if he wins."

He smiled, but his eyes didn't. "Now get going."

Jack stepped out of the car and walked through the crowd toward a cluster of public telephones, mounted in the center of the open-air lobby. It was a good idea Marcello had to make the call from the bus station. Buses in Brazil were what airplanes and trains were to the first world. Only the wealthy traveled often by plane. The bus was the workhorse of domestic transportation, and bus stations had nothing of the security at an airport. Jack was just one face in the mill with a thousand others, and dressed as he was—just a few miles from the Brazilian Army headquarters—he was one of at least a dozen officers awaiting friends or family from other far-flung parts of the country. But the real beauty of using the bus station as Marcello conceived it was that if the call was traced, the police would probably concentrate their net on roads leaving the capital. A person calling from a bus station was obviously on the move. Jack was glad to have a man who thought like Marcello on their side.

He stepped to a pay phone, pulled out the numbers he had copied from the phone book and dialed. After several rings a female voice came on the line, "*Embaixada dos Estados Unidos da America.*"

"Hello," Jack answered in English, "I would like to speak to the ambassador personally. My name is Jack Tate, the one in the news. I'll call back in two minutes." He hung up and walked across the lobby to another cluster of phones as Marcello instructed. When his time was up, he redialed. Again came the female voice, "Embaixada..."

"Is the ambassador on the line?"

"Yes, Mr. Tate. One moment please." The moment lasted over a minute. Jack timed it.

"Mr. Tate?"

"Ambassador?"

"Yes. This is Ambassador Phelps. You're in a lot of trouble, sir."

"It's not my fault, Mr. Ambassador. I've been framed."

"Framed? By who?"

"Senator Afonso Fonseca. He framed me with the murder of his son and Senhora Fontes, so he could have me killed by the police."

"These are serious charges. Do you have proof?"

"Yes, I do, Ambassador. I have a witness to the murder of Hernanie Fonseca who is willing to testify on my behalf, and I have tapes of computer files that detail a drug smuggling ring that the senator controls."

"Drug smuggling? Do you have those tapes with you?"

Jack didn't answer immediately. It seemed a strange question. Then he lied, "Yes, I have copies of them with me, Mr. Ambassador. The originals are in a safe place."

"And the girl, the one you are accused of kidnapping, is she with you?"

"Yes she is," Jack lied again. He looked at his watch—he had been on line for 3:45 seconds.

"I'll call you later, Ambassador."

"No, please, Mr. Tate. I need more. What kind of information do you have, exactly."

"I'll tell you about it later."

"Please, tell me now. It's important that I know."

"Later."

"No, Mr. Tate, don't hang up. Stay where you are. I'll have someone come by to pick you up. You are in great danger. Sit tight, and I'll send a car out now."

Jack hung up and walked briskly away to catch a cab, which he directed to the supermarket. As the cab mixed into traffic, he looked at the watch strapped to his shaking hand. The ambassador wasn't to be trusted. He'd tried to keep him on the line, just as Marcello said he might, and they had talked for four minutes and twelve seconds, just a bit over the limit. He hoped it hadn't been too much. The cab pulled into the busy parking lot of the large supermarket and left Jack at the front entrance. Marcello rolled up twenty seconds later.

"How did it go?" he asked

"Not good. I think they traced me."

"What makes you say that?"

"He told me that he was going to send somebody to pick me up, but I didn't tell him where I was."

"They made you all right."

Marcello pulled into a parking spot hidden among many other cars then popped open the trunk. "Get in, Jack. They might already have the road blocked."

With Jack hidden in the trunk, Marcello drove back onto the highway, but took a left away from the bus station heading the long way around the city. They were back at his apartment within twenty minutes.

He flipped on the TV as soon as they walked through the door, and they were greeted by Jack's smiling face, the picture from his visa application. It was replaced by one of Marisa. They were said to be both armed and very dangerous. Then the screen flashed to a live report from the bus station, which was crawling with police. Roadblocks had been placed on all highways leaving town, and airport security had been tripled.

Marcello sighed. "I'd better get you two out of here. It won't take them long to find out that Marisa is my niece and come looking for you here."

He mussed her hair while he rubbed his chin in thought. Then he smiled. "Come on, both of you. Get your bag of emeralds and help me pack a few things. I know just the place to hide you."

Chapter Eighteen

Marisa groaned when her feet touched the ground as her uncle helped her out of the trunk of the presidential limousine. Her legs were asleep and wobbly and full of the ringing sensation that lies somewhere between laughter and pain, definitely leaning toward pain. Jack unfolded himself and crawled out behind her. An hour of being luggage was more than enough for him. He arched backward, and his vertebrae popped themselves back in line.

"Have a nice trip?" asked Marcello.

"I've had better," answered Jack. "I thought you said this place was only forty minutes from your apartment."

"Traffic was tied up because of a roadblock. If I hadn't thought to use a presidential limo, they would have probably checked the trunk and found you. But these limos pass through anything. Wish I had one myself. You'll be safe here."

"Where are we?" asked Marisa, as she slowly put more weight on her feet, which were throbbing back to life.

"This is the *Granja do Torto*. It's a weekend house for the president."

He turned to Jack. "Sort of like your Camp David. It's perfect. The gate and the perimeter are manned by soldiers, and there isn't anybody else here, other than the groundskeepers and the cooks. There hasn't been a president who has used the place in over twenty years. Why would they, when they can get in the jet and fly to the beach, which is only an hour-and-a-half away? I think the expression in English for a place like this is 'Boondoggy,' isn't it, Jack?"

"Boondoggle, but it's a nice one. It's beautiful."

Jack and Marisa looked around. They were surrounded by a grove of tall, silvery-leafed eucalyptus trees, and in the distance, they could see a herd of fine horses grazing near a stable. Further on was the main house, well-kept and rustically beautiful, far different from what little of Brasília they had seen, which reminded Jack of a 1950s B-movie version of the Year 3,000—a collection of concrete and glass boxes marshaled into drill formation, a solitary government outpost six hundred miles from anywhere on a plain still mostly empty after 500 years of colonization. Brasília was an acquired taste, but this place had a rustic beauty. Jack was glad of the change.

"Help me with these groceries, Jack. We'd better go inside. I'd rather that the help didn't see you." Marcello, picked up two sacks and led them through the door.

"These are the quarters for the presidential guard. No one will bother you here." A small cloud of dust rose up when he set his bags down on the dining table. They all took a seat. Marcello ran his hand across the wood before him, and it came up red, coated with the clay dust endemic to the region. "You'll be safe enough here. It doesn't look like anyone's been in here to clean since the last rainy season. I hope the plumbing works."

"I'm not worried about the plumbing. I'm just glad to be alive," said Jack as he pulled the satchel from his shoulder and placed it on the table. "I can't thank you enough, Marcello, for helping us. You must be putting yourself in jeopardy by harboring fugitives."

"Forget it. Marisa is family, and I owe you a debt for helping her. But you are far from safe. We have to figure what to do to get you out of this."

"We could maybe hire a pilot to fly us out of the country through Amazonia up to Venezuela," offered Marisa. "Mato Grosso is full of bush pilots. There must be some around here."

"Sure," said her uncle. "But do you think any of them would risk a cargo like you two? They would lose their airplane and go to jail if they were caught. You're too hot, and besides what would you do once you got to Venezuela? She's one of Brazil's greatest trading partners. They would send you back in handcuffs. I'm afraid that even the U.S. would send you back, judging from the way your ambassador acted on the phone. The U.S. has been trying to get an extradition treaty with Brazil for years, and they might use you two as leverage to do it."

"What about the backup tapes?" asked Jack. "My government is very anti-drug."

"What did your ambassador say about them."

"Nothing, other than I was making serious allegations. I bet he'd believe me, though, if he saw them."

"He probably would, but I'm not sure that that would do you any good. He's been seen quite often with Fonseca over the last few months since *Presidente* Risolia started dropping in the polls. Fonseca's their favored candidate, and they might not want to depose him or gain his ill-will by going public with the information. This is the biggest economy on the continent, the eighth largest in the world. America might not want to jeopardize relations with Brazil even if she knew that the president was a drug dealer. Once he's in power, I doubt they would do anything other than slap his hands and tell him quietly to desist. They might even help him keep this secret. It might be in their interest to. Think about the possibilities of political blackmail if they had this to hold over him. They could pull his strings like a puppet."

"Good. Let them. I just want Marisa and I to be able to get out of this alive and with our emeralds." Jack opened the satchel and dumped its contents on the table—a rain of green crystals spilled out, as well as the computer tapes and the brick of cocaine that was still wrapped in the flour sack in which they'd found it. Jack picked up the largest emerald, the one Fonseca had wanted to keep for his wife, and held it to his eyes to rest them in its color. Marisa ran a hand absently through the other crystals while Marcello hefted the cocaine with a look of disgust.

"Filho-da-mãe."

He turned to spit, but didn't because they were inside.

"I went on at least a dozen raids on airstrips in Amazonia when I was in the special forces. We risk our lives to end this traffic in the jungle and nowadays, even in the cities, and this senator is one of the dealers. This is just too much! I wonder how many more there are like him. He can't become president. We can't let him. We have to stop the bastard and have to make him pay for killing my sister and Joaquim." He threw the cocaine down upon the table and brushed his hands off on his pants.

"What are we to do then?" asked Jack.

"I agree that the police are out of the question, and you could be right about the press and my government. They might sell us out to use our information as a bargaining chip, but then they might also protect us. They have a program for people who are witnesses against organized crime."

"Sure, anybody that watches TV knows about that, Jack, but would you really want to live that way? You'd have to disappear from everyone and everything you know. And how would Marisa get along in such a program in a foreign country where she doesn't even speak the language. She's not American. She's Brazilian."

"I could learn English, *Tio* Marcello."

"I'm sure you could, but you shouldn't have to. You haven't done anything wrong. You've been victimized enough. We need to be the aggressors from now on."

"What about the foreign press. I could give the files to some American journalists."

"But if you do that, you lose what security you have. You'd still be two potential witnesses that Fonseca would have to murder, and you'd still be fugitives from Brazilian justice. Having the story out on Fonseca wouldn't change that, not immediately anyway. If the police catch you, you're as good as dead, and even if the charges were dropped, he would still hunt you down. You know too much, not just about the drugs, but also about the death of his son. You could implicate him in that murder, as well as the murder of my sister and Joaquim and those other two men you found in the mine. Giving these files to the press would definitely hurt the senator, but I can't see it helping you." He picked up the tapes, weighing them in his hands, absently shuffling them back and forth.

"Well, what do you suggest?" asked Jack, whose gloom grew as their options diminished.

"I'll have to try to get them to the president."

"Can you do that for us, *tio*?" asked Marisa hopefully.

"I can try."

"You have access to him?" asked Jack.

"No, not really. Our job is to keep unauthorized people from getting access to him, and we take our job rather seriously. I'm a watch commander for the ground floor of the executive palace where the president works. We restrict the movement of people in and out of the building, but we don't directly protect the president. He has a staff of personal bodyguards that go wherever he goes, and those guys have orders to stop anyone who approaches him without authorization. They are good soldiers who know and like me, but I'm sure that they wouldn't let me get close without permission."

"Who could give you the permission?"

"Two people—my battalion commander and the president's chief of staff. But both of them are too political to trust with this information. The colonel wants to make general, so I doubt that he would risk offending Fonseca, who by most people's count will be our next president, and the chief of staff is said to be quietly seeking a position in the next administration. If I go to him with this, he could betray us and be named minister of foreign relations for his trouble."

"Well then, what do you plan on doing?" Jack asked as he put down the emerald and looked into the eyes of the major.

"I guess I'll just run up to the president when he gets inside the building with one of your tapes in hand, start shouting out everything you told me and pray that he'll hear me out."

"No, *tio*, you could lose your job and get in trouble."

He smiled and hugged her, "I swore to protect the country, not my pension. This will be the best thing I've ever done if I can do it. Who knows? I might even get a medal!"

He laughed, then again became serious.

"Look," he said. " If for some reason I can't get to him, you'd better get out of here. If you don't hear from me by midnight, leave.

"*Merda*, I should have thought to bring another car. Well, maybe you could steal one of the jeeps up by the gate, or you could take some horses if you had to."

"Why don't you put it off until tomorrow then?" asked Jack.

"No, today's the best day. I'm on the four to midnight shift, so I can catch him when he leaves his office to go home this evening. Tomorrow I'm off for two days, and then I go on the dog watch—midnight to eight. I'll be on it for three weeks and won't get off of it until after the election. It has to be today.

"Don't worry. I think he'll listen to me. He's a good man, and I've worked for him for over three years. It'll be all right, but just in case it's not, take these."

He stood and reached inside a grocery bag to withdraw two nine-millimeter automatics.

"And also take this."

He pulled a thick envelope from his coat pocket, which was stuffed with *cruzeiros reais*.

"It's about 3,500 dollars. I would give you more, but it's all I had in the bank. The rest of my money's squirreled away in investments, trying to beat inflation."

He handed it to Marisa, and she started to cry.

"Relax, little niece. It's just a precaution. Everything will be fine. Pray for that. I'd better get going. I have to get this car back to the motor pool and get to work in a little less than two hours. If you don't hear from me tonight, leave this place. Maybe you could try to get to Venezuela."

He hugged Marisa, shook Jack's hand and was quickly out the door, warming the car that he soon drove away. They went to the window and watched him leave, both filled with nervousness and a growing apprehension.

Chapter Nineteen

Marisa stood to clean away the dinner plates, but Jack motioned for her to stop.

"There's no reason to hurry through dinner, *querida*. Why don't we just sit here a minute and talk. Once dinner's over we won't have anything else to do. We don't even have a radio."

"I'd rather do them now, Jack. I want to keep busy."

"All right. Then let me help you with them."

He pushed his chair back and moved to get up.

"Please, Jack, you just sit there. Rest and drink your beer."

She put a hand on his shoulder, then drew it away quickly as if it were on fire. She hustled the dishes into the kitchen, which soon sounded with the splash of running water.

Jack sat back and felt a little hurt. She hadn't meant anything, he was sure. He understood, but he still ached whenever she drew away from him. He hadn't ever made a move to touch her, other to hug her when she cried. In fact, she was the one who often reached out to touch him, like she sometimes did during the nights in the boat or in the back of trucks when she would unconsciously roll into him as she slept, to pillow her head upon his shoulder.

But as soon as she awoke, she would jerk away from him and huddle into herself, pulling her knees to her chest and looking at him with wild, fright-filled eyes. She would recover in a moment and then often say something pleasant, but it still hurt him. He wondered if it would ever end, if she would ever get over it, and if she could ever love him the way he loved her.

Love him? It was sadly laughable. He was literally old enough to be her father, and the last several weeks hadn't done anything to make him younger. He cringed as he saw the man who looked back in the mirror when he showered in Marcello's apartment. His nose was now bent sharply to the left with a large hump lodged upon its bridge, and his still black-and-purple eyes made him look ghoulish. How could he even harbor the notion that she could somehow like him? It was ridiculous. But still, there was a bond between them that sprung from their common nightmare. They couldn't have survived without each other. And their futures were also linked—for the short term, anyway. He didn't quite know what it was, but he knew that they were family. He was really all she had left, other than her uncle whom she didn't really know. She was all he wanted.

He swallowed his warm beer and wondered what had happened to his life and if he would even have it in the morning. He looked at his watch—9:30 p.m. He hoped that Marcello would soon return. If not, they would have to leave at midnight. He got up and walked to the kitchen.

Marisa was drying the last dish when he entered. She smiled at him, but he could see that it was a mirthless smile. Her hands were shaking as she placed the plate in the drainer.

"What is it, Marisa? Why are you upset? Marcello's going to get us out of this. You know he will. He wouldn't try to get the president to help us if he didn't think he could.

From what I've seen of your uncle, he's not the kind of man who makes mistakes."

"But what if he does. What then? Then he'll get killed. You'll get killed, and that man will come to get me."

"The senator? Fonseca won't get you. I won't let him."

"You can't stop him. My father couldn't, my mother couldn't, and you can't either. He'll just take you from me like he took them, and then I won't have anyone left. He took everything, Jack. Don't you understand? He took everything I had in the world. And now he'll take you."

"I won't let him, Marisa. I'll kill him first. I should have killed him when I had the chance. I won't make that mistake again."

"No! He'll kill you. He'll kill you."

She broke down sobbing and rung the dishrag in her hands.

He walked up to her and tried to hug her, but she pulled away.

"Don't!"

She ran into the bathroom.

Jack stood there, dejected, listening to her cry from behind the closed door. Then slowly, he began packing their food back into the bags. It might have to last them a long time. Where would they go if Marcello didn't return? What chance would they have then? He sighed and wondered if it mattered. Then he took the bags into the living room and set them on the table, next to the pile of emerald rough stacked up like a pyramid to Oz.

Emeralds, his entire adult life he had searched for emeralds such as these, but now they weighed like marbles in his hand—not agates or any of the good ones that children covet and collect—more like the spheres of common glass abandoned in the sandbox with the light of dusk when mothers called their children in for supper.

Should men have died for these crystals? Should families have suffered? He thought of Marisa's father and of his friend. He thought of her mother and of Frau Klimt, to whom he'd have to break the news of her son if he lived. That poor, fat, jovial woman who seemed to spend her life in the kitchen cooking for her son. What could he say to comfort her? Who could she cook for now? The color of money caught in crystal had been the death of her son. Would it be her death, too? When would the old Parecis chief be satisfied? When would he end his curse? What had they to do with him or Chico Borba?

Jack swept the crystals back into the pouch and winced with the pain that shot out from his swollen thumb, and while he gathered the emeralds, he prayed. He wasn't very close to God before his jail time in Zaire and had seemed to have forgotten him once safely out of Africa, but he did believe. He prayed for an exit from their dilemma, and he prayed for the woman he loved, who in the short span of weeks had become more to him than anything, more than the wealth that he had spent a lifetime chasing and more than his own life. He prayed for her deliverance above all else.

It was then that he heard car engines.

Jack ran to the window in time to hear traffic at a distance, but near the gate. The horses heard it, too, and began snorting in the corral near the window. Why hadn't he taken the precaution to saddle a couple? He chastised himself bitterly.

"Marisa! Marisa!" He beat upon the bathroom door. "Marisa, we have to go! There are cars coming!"

She opened the door with horror in her eyes.

"They're coming?"

"Come on, *querida.*"

He pulled her from the doorway and handed her a pistol. "We've got to get out of here. Follow me."

He dragged her through the dining room, where he grabbed the satchel with their goods, then he pulled her through the back door, past the eucalyptus grove and toward the stables. As they ran through the dark, headlights surrounded the barracks that had been their refuge.

"Come on!" Jack helped her over the fence, and they were in with the horses. They made their way forward to the stables and hid inside a stall. "Stay here and keep quiet, and I'll try to find some saddles." He touched her chin and saw a flicker of the girl he knew flash in her eyes. She nodded bravely, and he crawled around the building, stumbling in the dark, groping for the livery that they needed.

Suddenly the stables were alive with light, angled down upon them.

"Halt! This is the Air Force! Lay down your arms and come out immediately!" sounded loudly above.

Jack ran back and pulled Marisa away from the window. Then he pulled the slide back on his pistol and motioned for her to do the same.

"Marisa, I want you to know one thing before I die," he cried above the swish of helicopter rotor blades.

"What's that, Jack?"

"I LOVE YOU!"

His voice was lost amid the roar of airborne turbines and the wash of spotlights.

Chapter Twenty

"Lay down your arms, and you will not be injured!" roared the loudspeaker above them.

Jack answered with a well-placed shot. Whether he hit the chopper or not he didn't know, but its engines screamed it away. Only headlights remained.

Fourteen bullets, Jack thought, fourteen left in mine and fifteen in hers. Twenty-seven for them and two for us. That's not bad. Marisa rose to look over the windowsill with him, but he pushed her down below.

"Lie down," he warned. "Or they'll shoot you."

He knelt there with his pistol at the ready, without a shot being fired either way for five minutes. It was a stand-off.

Finally, a lone figure approached them, hands in the air. Jack watched him come closer and squeezed-in on his trigger to the point of firing. The figure stopped less than twenty feet away.

"Jack, it's Marcello! Stop shooting! We're on your side!"

"Marcello?" shouted Jack, finger still tight on the trigger.

"Who did you think, Carmen Miranda?"

"It's my uncle!" said Marisa, who started to stand.

"Get down!" Jack pushed her into the hay. "Come on forward, but keep your hands held high. If you move, you're dead."

The figure kept approaching until it stood a foot in front of Jack's raised pistol, obscuring him from snipers.

"*Meu Deus*, Jack," said Marcello, "You don't joke around do you?"

"We got this far, didn't we?"

"Yes, you did, but why are you shooting at us? I told you I'd be back before midnight!"

"But you didn't say anything about bringing the Air Force with you."

"We're here to protect you."

Jack rose and stuck the pistol under Marcello's chin.

"You sure about that?"

"Jack, I could have killed you when we met, remember?"

Jack lowered his gun.

"Sorry."

"Forget about it. Now give me those pistols. I have brought somebody here who wants to talk to you, if you haven't already killed him."

Marisa stood and hugged her uncle, then she and Jack handed over their pistols.

"Thanks," said Marcello. "You scared the shit out of me!"

Then he spoke into the walkie-talkie that was strapped on his shoulder, "This is X-RAY KILO ALPHA. The Choir is singing. Repeat, the choir is singing!"

"Roger that X-RAY KILO ALPHA. We're on our way back."

"The choir is singing?" asked Jack to the major who was motioning to the men behind the cars that the action was over.

"It was the best I could do in a hurry," he answered over his shoulder. "I sing in church on Sundays."

In minutes, the helicopter was back, but this time it landed.

"Follow me!"

He led them to the center of the horse pasture where the chopper set down. As soon as the skids hit the ground, four large men in business suits scrambled out, all waving machine pistols. Marcello marched up to them hands in the air and was soon frisked and relieved of his three pistols. Jack and Marisa were then also frisked. When the leader of the team nodded his satisfaction to the pilot, the door opened and two other bodyguards jumped out, followed by Wilson Risolia, the president of the Federative Republic of Brazil.

The president stepped to Marcello and said, "I must tell you, major, that was the most exciting flight of my life. A bullet passed through the cockpit just above the pilot."

"Forgive me, *Senhor Presidente*!" said an embarrassed Marcello. "I should have disarmed them first. They were nervous."

"That's understandable. Major, if what you've told me is true, you'll be the youngest general in the Army. Now, introduce me."

"Mr. President, this is my niece, *Senhorita* Marisa da Silva Fontes, and this is her friend, Mr. Jack Tate of the United States."

"*Senhorita* Fontes, I'm charmed." He kissed her cheeks.

"Likewise, *Senhor Presidente*!"

"And Mr. Tate." He spoke in perfect East Coast English. "It's always a pleasure to meet a foreigner so interested in our country."

He gave Jack a firm handshake.

"The pleasure's mine, *Senhor Presidente*. I'm honored to meet you, sir," said Jack, who grimaced because of his damaged thumb.

"Please, let's get out from under these rotor blades," said President Risolia.

He led them toward the presidential summer house, which hadn't seen a president in recent memory. When they entered the house, a butler and a flurry of maids rushed around nervously to attend the man whom they were there to serve, but who never came. He dismissed them, and then ushered Jack, Marisa, Marcello and a handsome gray-haired man into a private office, leaving his bodyguards outside the door.

"Mr. Tate, *Senhorita* Fontes, this is General Ribeiro, the chief of our national intelligence agency." The general shook their hands. "General Ribeiro has studied some of the data contained in the computer tape that you gave us, and he thinks that it is legitimate."

"Yes, I do," said the general. "Unfortunately, the tape was water damaged, but we have managed to extract a few files that I think show a link to some cocaine seizures in Rio de Janeiro. The delivery dates on the tape correspond to our seizures…to the day. These were small seizures made on three separate occasions when drug smugglers were arrested at roadblocks leaving the industrial sector of the city. The cocaine was packaged similarly to the brick your uncle brought us. We haven't been able to locate this distribution source in Rio, but from the amount of cocaine we seized, we always thought it to be big. The tape shows it to be even bigger than we imagine, around a ton a month. The major said you have another tape."

"Yes we do. It's in the satchel." He pointed to their satchel, which Marcello had taken with the guns. Marcello dug it out and handed it to General Ribeiro.

"Good. If this tape is intact, we should be able to break one of the biggest drug smuggling operations in the country, and we can keep Senator Fonseca from winning the presidency. How on earth did you get these tapes?"

"The major has explained that briefly to me, general," said President Risolia.

He looked to Jack and Marisa, and said, "But I would like to hear it from you in more detail. How did you become involved with Senator Fonseca?"

Jack took the heavy satchel from Marcello and dumped it on the table. The president and the general stared down at the pile of crystals heaped before them.

"*Meu Deus,* that must be a fortune!" gasped the wide-eyed general.

"I'd guess between ten and twenty million dollars once it's cut," said Jack. "This large one could be worth over two million by itself, if it's as clean inside as it looks to be."

He handed the large, green hexagon to the president, who hefted it as he sat down behind the unfamiliar desk. He motioned for them to sit also.

"The general and I are listening."

So Jack and Marisa told their tale, beginning with Jack's search for her father. He did most of the talking, but she often broke in to punctuate his narrative with facts he omitted and with clarifications. After he had spoken for about five minutes, he mentioned their capture and his return to the mine where Fonseca had ordered him to be buried alive.

"Why did Fonseca send you back to the mine alone without Marisa?" asked General Ribeiro.

The president saw the change of expression in Marisa. It was answer enough.

"That's not important for the moment, general. Please continue, Mr. Tate."

Marisa looked relieved.

Jack spoke on about his return to the ranch and their escape through the Pantanal, across the border to Bolivia, and their ride back into Brazil and ultimately to Brasília. He omitted the details of Marisa's rapes, and though he thought they all noticed gaps in his story, none of them mentioned it.

When he ended the story with the phone call to his ambassador and their journey to the *Granja do Torto* in the back of a presidential limousine, neither the president nor the general spoke. They looked at the two fugitives with something akin to respect or awe in their eyes. It was obvious that both of these powerful men thought that Jack and Marisa had done very well to have survived their ordeal.

When the president finally spoke, he did so with a hint of a smile—his political fortunes had changed. He knew then that the presidency would be his again for another four years, and this time, without Fonseca at the head of the coalition that blocked him in the senate, he would finally be able to implement the economic and social policies that he hoped would spark the transformation of his country from a disparate coalition of backwater fiefdoms into a prosperous nation.

He sat in silence and contemplated how best to use the explosives set before him to bring down the house of Fonseca. It would be tricky this close to election time with Fonseca so far in the lead. But the evidence was irrefutable, and he would be a hero in the end.

"*Senhorita* Fontes, Mr. Tate, I am impressed and can assure you that I will work to get you out of the legal trouble you are in, and that you will have the mineral rights for your mine, if you are willing to help me to put the senator in jail."

"Of course we'll help you, *Senhor Presidente!*" Marisa almost shouted.

"We'll do anything you ask of us, sir," said Jack.

"You do realize that this will result in a criminal trial, in which everything that happened to you will probably come out? It could be very painful."

He looked into Marisa's eyes.

She glanced away but answered, "That doesn't matter. I want to see him pay for everything he's done to me and to my family."

"He will pay, *Senhorita*. He'll pay with every day of life left to him."

She looked up. "He should."

"We will punish him with the full measure of the law. Of that, you can be sure."

The president stood. "Let's get back to Brasília. There is much to be done in the next few days."

They followed him to the door, where he stopped for a moment to ask, "Tell me, *Senhorita*, have you ever been on television?"

Chapter Twenty-one

The corridors of *TV Nacional* were already alive that morning with the crazed hurry of the week before the national elections. Senators and congressmen hustled in and out of the studio followed by shouted questions from reporters and the flash of cameras, which lent the place a *Carnaval* air.

Into this madness strode the *Presidente da República* in the company of General Ribeiro and Minister of Justice Aurélio Marconi. Jack and Marisa came in behind them, surrounded by a cordon of plainclothes military and federal police. Studio One, their destination, was a large sound stage rigged for political announcements normally used by the president himself or by members of his cabinet. It was also used by other high-powered politicians, including Senator Afonso Fonseca de Cabral, who was in it just then, taping a campaign commercial to be aired that evening during the mandatory political hour. They walked into the studio, even though the red light was on, and stood quietly in the wings to listen to his bombast.

"So I ask you, people of Brazil, are you ready for another four years of do-nothing government? Has anything changed in the last four years? Are you any better off than you were before? You're not. Demand change! Demand a better life! That is what I am demanding and it is what I have been demanding for you the last four years as leader of the opposition. Let me steer this country into the future! Let's not wallow in the misery that President Risolia has cast us all. Look at what has become of our country! Drug wars in the *favelas*! Robbery in the streets! We can't let this continue! We must stop this madness before your children go the way of my poor, poor son Hernanie! If I was president, by God, the murderer of my boy would be in prison and not roaming unhindered around our streets like he is today. Throw out Risolia. End this madness! Vote Fonseca! Vote for a change! Vote for a chance! VOTE FOR A MAN!"

With that, the camera stopped rolling and Fonseca stood to be washed with congratulations by his campaign staffers. They followed him to the door, where he was startled to see President Risolia. He grimaced, then walked up to him, not offering to shake hands.

"What are you doing here, *Senhor Presidente*?" He smiled darkly then added, "But not president for long, eh?"

"Oh I don't know, Afonso. I might stay on a bit longer than you think. If I were you, I'd pay close attention to the polls from now until election day."

Fonseca glowered, "What are you talking about? I'm destroying you."

"Maybe for the moment, but that doesn't concern me very much. Oh, by the way, I brought someone with me whom you've been looking for.

"Jack and Marisa, would you come over here please?"

The police escort stepped aside to reveal Jack and Marisa, who had been obscured behind them.

Fonseca's jaw dropped and his eyes widened with hostility and disbelief.

"You? You? Again!"

Jack stepped forward, but Marisa stayed where she was.

"That's right, senator. It's us again. You should have let us go when I gave you the chance. Now you're going to have to pay for that."

Hate played in Fonseca's eyes.

"I don't know what you are talking about, you murderer."

Then Fonseca's tone changed as he turned back to face the president. "It's good that you have caught them, Wilson. I was afraid that they were going to escape the country."

"Well, I didn't exactly catch them, Afonso. The fact is, they came to me. They have filed some very serious charges against you, senator."

"Charges! You let wanted criminals file charges against the president-elect of Brazil?"

"The election's not until Wednesday, but I can see your point—I suppose if I were you, I would find that odd too. But you see, they brought me something that corroborates their story. General Ribeiro, would you please give the senator a copy of the press release."

The general pulled a sheaf of papers from his briefcase and handed them to Fonseca, who paled as he scanned through them.

"What have you done?" he asked darkly, choking on his rage. "How could you do this to me? I am a Fonseca!"

He lunged at the president, whose ever present bodyguards intercepted him and held him firmly.

"You might be a Fonseca, but you are also a murderer, a drug trafficker and a traitor to your country. And you are under arrest. A senator selling drugs like a common criminal—you should be executed. You disgust me."

He motioned to the guards and said, "Take this man away and hand him over to the federal police outside."

Fonseca struggled against them and railed against the president as they dragged him out the door.

President Risolia turned to Marisa and said, "I don't know if I should have let you witness that scene or not, but I wanted you to know that your family's murder will not go unpunished. The senator will never see the light of day again. That, I can promise."

"Thank you, *Senhor Presidente*. That makes me happy."

"Good! Well then, everyone, let's begin the news conference."

As they were led to their places by the station manager, a long line of reporters filed in to take seats in rows before them. When the camera's light blinked on, the president, flanked by Minister Marconi and General Ribeiro, addressed his nation:

"*Senhores e Senhoras*, citizens of Brazil, it is with great sadness that I make this announcement, which is certain to shock our nation and its confidence in our government.

"At midnight last night, elements of the 9th and 15th Army Special Forces battalions parachuted into a ranch a few hundred kilometers south of Cuiabá where they were met by federal police officers on the ground, whom they joined in a combined operation. They discovered over two tons of cocaine, a cache of stolen military arms—those stolen from the Navy arsenal in Rio last year—and they also seized computer documentation of the largest cocaine smuggling operation ever uncovered in Brazil, an operation with tentacles spreading all the way to the United States, Great Britain and France. Similar operations were conducted simultaneously by those countries, and by our Army and police in Rio and São Paulo, where more drugs and arms were found. Over 150 drug traffickers were arrested last night, and other known suspects are being searched for this morning.

"Unfortunately, this great strike against the trade in illicit drugs, which has been crippling our cities. was not without its price. Four soldiers were killed in the line of duty, and another three were seriously injured. The nation owes a debt to these fine young men, and we will feel their loss. I have declared tomorrow to be a National Day of Mourning for these heroes, and all flags shall fly at half-staff in tribute to them.

"The most troubling aspect of this vicious ring was not its huge proportions, or even the fact that our soldiers died destroying it. Those brave young men paid the highest price, but it was worth it because in doing so, they saved our nation from possibly traveling down a steep path to darkness, for the leader and apparent mastermind of this despicable ring was Afonso Fonseca de Cabral, senator and candidate for the presidency."

There was an immediate roar of questions from the reporters. The president held up a hand for silence.

"I will soon give the floor to Minister Marconi, who will explain the military strikes in detail, and then to General Ribeiro, who will describe the evidence that led us to break this ring, but please, let me continue.

"To discover a criminal in such a high government post is shocking to all of us, but it should not shake your belief in our system of government. The system does work. It works well. This will be the third federal election since the end of military rule ten years ago. We, as a people, are capable of democratic self-government. No one wants to turn back the clock, so in view of this distressing news, I ask you simply to consider the candidates carefully and make solid, informed choices.

"Senator Fonseca is now being charged and will be held in prison until a judge determines if he may be released on bail, but he is still a candidate and his name cannot be removed from the ballot until he has been convicted. Please listen carefully to what Minister Marconi and General Ribeiro have to say and read the evidence, which we will give to the media immediately after this press conference. It is your duty as citizens to know the candidates and their platforms, and it is your duty to elect the best possible government for our nation. I hope that you choose well.

"One last thing I should mention, before I take any questions, is about some upsetting news that we have all been watching closely over the last few days—about the accused murderer, Jack Tate, who has been supposedly holding a woman hostage as he tried to escape from Brazil. Well, it turns out that Mr. Tate is not a murderer, and his supposed hostage, Marisa Fontes, wasn't a hostage at all. They were both fleeing from Senator Fonseca, who was trying to kill them for legally mining on his property. The senator killed *Senhorita* Fontes' father, her mother and two other men to keep the mine unexploited, so the secret of his smuggling operation would remain safe. Beyond murder, this in itself is a crime. You can't deny legitimate industry to a poor people. Our mining laws ensure that anyone who finds minerals can mine them unless they happen to be on Indian lands. Many men could make their living mining for emeralds on the *Fazenda* Fonseca, but the senator prevented that to protect his own illegal interests. Well, that will no longer be the case. I am opening the legendary Borba mine to the people of Brazil and will now stand as witness while Marisa Fontes files her legal claim."

The Minister of Mining and Energy led Marisa to the podium, where he and the president witnessed her signing of the register.

When she was done, President Risolia kissed her on the cheeks and said, "*Senhorita* Fontes, you have served your country well by bringing the crimes of *Senador* Fonseca to light and for pioneering emerald mining in the Pantanal. Brazil salutes you."

She smiled, and then she and the minister walked back into the wings while the president began fielding questions from the horde of headline-hungry reporters.

"Well," said Jack as she stepped, beaming, toward him. "It looks like your dreams are going to come true after all, Marisa. You're a millionaire now, and the apartment in Leblon is yours for the choosing. Everything you ever wanted is going to be yours."

He smiled warmly, but in the warmth, there was a current of sadness. He felt a sense of loss, knowing they were finally safe and that their adventure had come to a close. He mused that he would soon see the day when his only contact with her would be in trading-in her emeralds. That's all he had wanted just a short month before, but at the moment, it meant nothing.

He didn't care if he ever saw another emerald again. She was what he wanted, and he knew he wasn't going to get her. So much for happy endings.

He looked at her, dressed simply in the white dress the presidential tailor had managed to fit her for, in just one short hour. Even with her bruises, she seemed so beautiful to him that it hurt.

"You will certainly enjoy Leblon. You'll have a good life there. I'm sure of it."

"I don't know anyone there or anything about the place, really. I guess I'll go there, though, because of *Mamãe's* dream. That's what she wanted."

"You'll meet plenty of people willing to show you everything about it, *querida*. Believe me on that! Go there and live your mother's dream. It's your dream too, remember?"

"I know it is, but do you remember your promise, Jack? You said you were going to take me to the beach yourself and show me around."

"No, I didn't forget. I'd love to be the one who shows you Rio for the first time. It will be a magic moment for you, and I'd like to share in it."

"Good, I want you to, but we have to go shopping first."

"Shopping? For what?"

"Some nice dresses, jeans and a new bikini, maybe in a nice emerald green. Would you help me pick one out?"

She looked into his eyes, and he stared deep in hers— they were still glassy with the torture and the sadness held within her, but there was something else, too.

She rose up on the balls of her feet and brushed him lightly on the lips. "I just need time, Jack. Okay?"

He hugged her to him tightly and believed again in happy endings.

-The End-

About the Author

B rian Ray Brewer is an author and inventor with many patents to his credit. He was once a merchant seaman, a naval officer, a jeweler, an EMT and an engineer who worked in South American oilfields and power plants. Brian lives with his wife and daughters on water in Brazil.

Author's Education:

United States Merchant Marine Academy:

BS, Marine Engineering & Marine Transportation, 1987.

Gemological Institute of America: Graduate Gemologist, 1995.

California State University, Dominguez Hills: MA, Humanities, 1999.

Harvard University Extension School: ALM, Creative Writing and Literature, 2022.

Books by this Author

Novels

The Face of God
Emerald Greed
Bilongo
The Diving God
The Rapture (Coming in 2023)
Perdition (Coming in 2024)

Poetry

From a Seaman to his Wife
Cries Primeval

CPSIA information can be obtained
at www.ICGtesting.com
Printed in the USA
BVHW082340270421
605943BV00007B/499